Opportunity

Office Roulette, Book Three

Kennedy Layne

OPPORTUNITY

Dedication

Jeffrey—To the best research partner in crime…we make a great team!

Cole—There are so many opportunities in front of you…make the best choices!

USA Today Bestselling Author Kennedy Layne brings you the thrilling conclusion to the Office Roulette trilogy...

Gareth Nicollet had been born into wealth, but he'd learned at an early age that money wasn't everything it was cracked up to be. Regrettably, he'd made a meaningful choice early on in his life that now threatened his future with the woman he loved.

Cynthia Ellsworth valued many things, but trust and loyalty were at the top of her list. She'd always known the man who shared her bed had secrets, but she never thought in a million years that he had the ability to destroy her career and her heart with a single blow.

Someone once said that greed was balanced by fear, but that wasn't entirely true when there was nothing left to lose. Unfortunately, Gareth's secret is the very reason the roulette wheel is spinning and Cynthia's life hangs in the balance.

CHAPTER ONE

"STEVE, YOU CAN'T order this gift for the client."

Cynthia Ellsworth made her way across the trading room floor with her favorite pair of black high heels clicking precisely the way she wanted. She'd purposefully pulled them out of the back of her closet for this purpose. The designer shoes were like battle gear to her, and she needed all the ammunition she could get, today of all days.

"Why?"

"Did you really just have the audacity to ask me that?" Cynthia's steel tone got Steve Lewis to turn around in his desk chair. She understood that he was busy and in the middle of the stock market's opening, but that didn't mean she would allow him to cut corners. The last thing this firm needed was to raise another red flag. "I can actually see those little black squirrels in your head running a million miles an hour on that treadmill. You've got less than zero chance of putting one over on me. You know the SEC rules regarding gifts, as well as our own compliance regulations. You'll have to choose another gift with a lesser value."

"The gift is only a few dollars over the usual acceptable tolerance." Steve went back to monitoring his screens, as if her role here at Manon Investments wasn't as esteemed as his. She'd already had a hell of a morning. This situation was something she could nip in the bud, which she fully intended to do. "Jerry and Darla are getting married next month. I'm sure you can figure out a way to skirt the rules."

"Oh, really?" Cynthia asked, tacking on a bit of syrupy inference to her words. She was quicker than he was when it came to answering one of the many ringing lines. He came up short when she leaned down and managed to set the palm of her hand over the receiver before him. "I'm glad to see I now have your attention, Steve. In case you've forgotten, my role here as compliance officer is to protect the firm—unfortunately, that includes protecting you from yourself. So, you *are* going to pick another gift to give Jerry and his future wife or you're going to pay for it out of your own pocket like any true friend would do under normal circumstances."

Cynthia didn't wait for Steve to acknowledge her request as she walked away.

Okay, it wasn't a request, but she didn't have the patience to draw out a heated debate knowing full well she would win in the end. Besides, she'd spent the past hour taking care of smaller issues that had risen this morning. She had more important things on her to-do list.

It was finally time for her to focus on the issue that had kept her up most of the night.

"Cynthia?" Marilyn called out from her seat behind the reception desk, preventing Cynthia from walking to her office. The older woman was in her sixties and the glue that held this company together. "Paul called in and said to tell you that he's running a few minutes late."

Of course.

Why wouldn't Paul be running late today of all days?

The universe had been conspiring against Cynthia for the past eight months. She hadn't known about that bit of treachery until yesterday, but it had been there all the same.

"Thank you, Marilyn." Cynthia managed a smile, not wanting to take her bad mood out on the older woman. Steve had been another matter altogether. "Would you please let me know when Paul comes in?"

Marilyn nodded her response, but it was clear that she had something else to say. She leaned forward so that her words didn't carry outside the large foyer. Cynthia's stomach knotted, because now wasn't the time for the mother hen to smooth over ruffled feathers. She was wasting her time.

Nothing could be said or done to ease Cynthia's pride at being duped by a man she'd thought was better than the rest.

Gareth Nicollet had pretty much brought her to her knees, and she'd been the one to give him that power on a silver platter. Apparently, she'd even tied a bow around the fucking thing.

Why was it that the most important lessons were always the hardest to learn?

"You know that Steve is having a hard time." Marilyn gave a rather sad smile, conveying the remorse that most of the employees were dealing with at the moment. Was it wrong that Cynthia didn't care about any of them when her own heart had all but been ripped to shreds? "He's just trying to—"

"Steve had an affair with his boss' ex-wife, lied to his former colleague and friend, and then attempted to taint my reputation in front of the entire staff not even three weeks past." Cynthia could go on and on about Steve's behavior over the last month, but it would have been a useless endeavor. She was just grateful for the sliver of anger that pushed aside the hurt. "Look, you and I both know that Steve is most likely moving to London to work with his brother-in-law when Manon investments closes its doors. So save the drama. Honestly, I think that's the wisest choice, but that doesn't mean he gets a free pass to do as he pleases until that eventuality."

Cynthia was saved from another lecture delivered by Marilyn when Laurel Calanthe and Grace Dorrance breezed through the glass entry doors from the elevator bank. Her two best friends must have gone downstairs to the café to caffeinate themselves, because Laurel was holding a smoothie in her left hand that clearly wasn't hers. The woman was a coffee drinker through and through. She'd have an IV installed if it were medically possible.

"Looks like we're just in time," Laurel said with a tentative smile that was meant for Marilyn. "Cynthia hasn't had her protein smoothie this morning. You know how she gets."

"I'm standing right here in front of you," Cynthia responded wryly, not wanting to get dragged into Laurel's office for a pep talk that was only going to make things worse. "Remind me why we're friends?"

"Because you have the keys to the gates of hell," Grace called out without hesitation as she continued to walk toward Laurel's office. "We wouldn't want to be left standing out in the cold."

"Come on," Laurel encouraged as she handed over the smoothie. Cynthia's stomach revolted, but she took the cold beverage anyway. "Let's go into my office and walk through what you're going to say to Gareth."

"Marilyn, I'll be in Laurel's office. Please let me know the moment Paul walks through those doors." Cynthia fell into step beside Laurel as they both slowly followed Grace down the corridor. "Laurel, I've already decided not to say anything to Gareth, and I don't want to argue about it anymore. I'm dumping this entire situation into Paul's lap later this morning before washing my hands of it. Then I can finally move on with my life."

Cynthia didn't miss Laurel's quick glance toward the corner

office door at the end of the hallway, so she most likely hadn't heard a word that was said. Her friend's revolted shudder was more than evident, but Cynthia couldn't blame her after what had taken place.

"It's probably a good thing we're moving offices at the beginning of the year." Cynthia hated that Laurel had to continually see the place where she'd found their boss—Brad Manon—murdered with his throat cut a little over three weeks ago. It couldn't have been healthy to look at that view numerous times a day. "A fresh start is exactly what we all need."

"What you need is to find out why Gareth Nicollet didn't tell you the truth about being Brad Manon's brother," Grace interjected from her seat on Laurel's credenza as she waited for them to cross the threshold. "None of us believe that Gareth is capable of murder, but he obviously kept his family relationship with Brad a secret for a reason. You need to find out why exactly that is."

"No, I don't." Cynthia ignored the throbbing pain in her chest. She was a business professional. She had known better than to mix business with pleasure, but she'd done it anyway. Now it was time to pay the piper. "As I was just telling Laurel, I'm meeting with Paul the moment he sees fit to get his ass into the office today. He can make any decisions that need to be made regarding Gareth. I'm out."

Cynthia reluctantly took a seat in one of Laurel's guest chairs, crossing her legs and smoothing the material of her black skirt. When was the last time any of them had a conversation that didn't involve any one of them or their colleagues going to prison?

Far too damn long, that's when.

It was all Laurel's fault. She just had to come into the office three weeks ago at some ungodly hour to grab some stupid files.

Leave it to her to stumble upon Brad's dead body and unknow-ingly set all their lives on a collision course for the deepest pit of hell.

It was times like these that unfortunate secrets were revealed and lives were ruined.

These days, it seemed like everyone and their uncle had something to hide.

The police certainly weren't lacking for suspects in Brad's murder. Almost every employee had the means, motive, and opportunity to commit the gruesome act according to the record thus far. The changes in Brad's personality over the years hadn't gone unnoticed by many, and the man had basically become isolated in that corner office as a result of his own actions.

It only seemed fitting that he'd died there in a cell of his making, but Cynthia wasn't known for her tact. She told it like it was, and she didn't harbor any regrets.

Well, sometimes.

Very few.

Other colleagues weren't so blunt, and that was part of the problem. It was hard to tell where people stood in the grand scheme of things. Not that they had to declare their allegiances, for fuck's sake.

Take Paul Slater, for instance. He'd been Brad's best friend and business partner. Over the years, Paul had spent more of his time out of the office persuading high net worth individuals to invest their money in Manon Investments than he had in the office dealing with Brad's insolence over minor issues that could be mitigated by others.

Then there was Steve Lewis, the head trader she'd had to deal with a few minutes ago. He'd been having an affair with Meredith Manon and keeping that little secret from his best friend and colleagues, not that it was technically any of their business. Normally, no one cared who was sleeping with who, but when it involved the ex-wife of the once beloved boss…well, people tended to get their hackles up in situations like that.

Speaking of the recent ex-widow, it wasn't like she was inheriting a fortune, considering Brad had been in massive debt at the time of his death. Still, the police always seemed to suspect the spouse…or ex-spouse, in cases like these.

Then there were the conflicting motives of Vern Roberts, Blair Holmes, Phil Colbert, Joshua Green, Marilyn Kent, Smith Gallo, the two ladies currently in this office, and quite a few others. As a matter of fact, all of those individuals were just some of the employees who met all three of the criteria to commit murder.

"You've been seeing Gareth Nicollet on and off for close to a year," Laurel said, taking a seat in her desk chair as she set a sympathizing gaze on Cynthia. She didn't bother to correct her friend by saying it had only been eight months. Her speaking would only drag out this conversation, but it did take all her effort not to snap at her friend. Both Laurel and Grace were only trying to help. Unfortunately, there was nothing that could ease the pain of betrayal Cynthia was currently suffering at the glaring omission manifested by the man she'd fallen in love with. "Your instincts are better than both of ours. You can't tell us that you think Gareth is capable of murder."

"I never dreamed he would deceive me, either," Cynthia countered sharply, wincing when her anger slipped through her composure. She was fully aware that the employees of Manon Investments weren't the only suspects the police had on their rather large list. And now it was she who was liable for adding another name to the catalog of suspects. "Look, I appreciate what you two are trying to do right now. I really do, but nothing can erase the fact that Gareth kept the truth from me from the very start."

Cynthia didn't even bother to bring Brad into the equation. Hell, the police were likely to include her name in the pool after discovering that Brad hadn't seen fit to tell her that he was related to Gareth—a client, for that matter.

It was now official.

The throbbing in her temples had now become a full-fledged headache.

"In case you forgot, I was falsely accused of murdering Brad," Grace said while sharing a concerned glance with Laurel. "Detective Nielsen arrested me in front of all my friends and colleagues. It was beyond humiliating. You coming clean about Gareth's connection to Brad might very well lead the police to you. Don't you realize your own situation? It gives both of you motive."

Cynthia's hands had been cold since yesterday, when she'd discovered Gareth's lie in Brad's personnel file. She must have stared in horror at that seemingly inconsequential piece of information for at least ten minutes before she'd accepted it as truth. As it stood, she didn't need the added chill from the smoothie, so she set the plastic cup on Laurel's desk before curling her fingers into her palms.

"I know exactly what Gareth's omission has done to the both of us, but covering up for someone is exactly what got you arrested in the first place."

None of them had been overlooked by Detective Nielsen.

Laurel was the first to be questioned, and not just for the reason that she'd found Brad dead in his office. She'd been having an affair with Smith Gallo, another employee and the man with whom she'd been competing in regard to partnership at the firm. Both of them had been under scrutiny, especially when the police discovered that Smith had been planning to leave Manon Investments in order to open his own hedge fund.

Neither Cynthia nor Laurel had known at the time that Grace had given a false alibi for the timeframe of Brad's death. She'd lied to protect the man she was seeing—Rye Marshall—who just happened to be Manon Investments' largest competitor.

The killer had obviously discovered Grace's attempt to protect Rye, because a knife had been planted inside of her vehicle. An anonymous call had led the police straight to Grace's doorstep—or in this case, to the offices of Manon Investments.

Whoever was responsible for Brad's death was connected to all of them in some way or another, giving that individual the advantage. That specific detail told her that this wasn't a circumstance to be trifled with, which was why she was washing her hands of the entire situation.

"Grace isn't saying that you should lie." That was exactly what their friend was suggesting, but Laurel ignored the obvious. "Having been in similar situations, we're suggesting that speaking with Gareth before you talk to anyone else might be in both your best interests."

"Similar situations?" Cynthia slowly stood, not wanting to take her anger out on the two people who had her back in this cutthroat business. She fully understood that her friends were trying their best to help her deal with the fallout of a relationship that never should have begun in the first place, but they were going about it the wrong way. "You seem to be forgetting something rather important, ladies. The men in your lives never lied to you about who they were. Now as I stated earlier, I'm dumping this police matter into Paul's inbox and washing my hands of this whole problem."

Cynthia sensed Gareth's presence before either of her

friends glanced toward the doorway in shock. She wasn't sure how to explain it, but a blanket of warmth always came over her when he was in the vicinity. The fact that he could still have that effect on her after what he'd done gave her the internal fortitude to compose herself.

Hell would freeze over before she ever showed Gareth Nicollet that he still had the power to destroy her heart. Bracing herself, she straightened her shoulders before turning on the heels that had gotten her through many power struggles. Unfortunately, he gained the upper hand when he spoke first.

"Do you think it's going to be that easy to get rid of me, Cyn?"

CHAPTER TWO

IT WAS RARE that Gareth Nicollet ever wanted for anything.

He hadn't needed to.

He'd been adopted by loving parents as an infant, he had siblings who loved him despite his flaws, and he had more money in his numerous bank accounts than he could ever spend in two lifetimes. He also never lacked for a woman's company at night, let alone a cold one.

That was, until recently.

Cynthia Ellsworth wasn't just any woman, though. Not quite. She was intelligent, witty, confident, and downright stunningly beautiful—beyond compare. Her hair was blacker than the darkest raven, her complexion was as flawless as the finest porcelain, and her bone structure of those flushed cheeks reminded him of those marble statues in his favorite piazza in Florence. She was a masterpiece, and she'd been warm and inviting…until now.

Unfortunately, Cynthia wasn't faking the anger radiating so recently from those startling blue eyes of hers. There only was one reason she would be this upset with him, and that was if she'd discovered that dusty skeleton in his familiar closet.

Damn it.

He should have seen this coming and taken the preventative steps to avoid this upcoming confrontation by simply telling her the truth.

"Could we speak in private?" Gareth never took his eyes off Cynthia, wanting to ensure that he caught every emotion that crossed her lovely features. "Please."

And there it was. She'd blinked away the flicker of hurt as quickly as it had appeared, but he'd seen it nonetheless.

It had never been his intention to keep his past hidden from her forever, but he'd learned early on to protect himself due to his family's wealth. The progression of a relationship was meant to slowly unravel such situations, anyway. He'd known without a doubt that Cynthia was someone special within those first few days over eight months ago, but he hadn't wanted to ruin their newfound rapport by dropping a bomb. After all, he'd already been fighting against the drawback of being one of her firm's clients. He didn't need to add to the negative side of the balance sheet.

Gareth hadn't gotten this far in his life without learning to deal with these types of problems in their own time. Unfortunately, he'd run out of that precious commodity, and now it was doubtful that Cynthia would believe he was ever going to tell her about his connection to Brad Manon.

"Cynthia?"

She'd taken her sweet time answering, and he discreetly breathed a sigh of relief when she took a determined step forward. He should have known there was a catch.

"You have two minutes to state your position."

Gareth instinctively stepped back into the hallway to let Cynthia pass. Her seductive perfume practically laid a trail for him to follow, but he wasn't foolish enough to think this upcoming confrontation was going to be very pleasant. He decided to first tackle the initial problem that led her to seek out time to herself, postponing what was to be a hell of a showdown.

"I didn't expect to receive a phone call from you while I was in Dubai telling me that you needed time to think things through. I must have misunderstood." Gareth had fallen into step with Cynthia, whose long legs certainly matched his own stride. She was tall, and her high heels put her almost at eye level with him…almost. "I thought we were past that particular stage."

Cynthia didn't respond to his bait, but instead continued down the hallway and out into the foyer. Marilyn was smart enough not to mention the fact that she'd told him to wait for Cynthia in her office, because neither he nor Cynthia needed reminding that he was one of Manon Investments' clients.

Technically, it hadn't been in either of their best interests to become involved as they had.

It was too late to go back and change the course of their budding relationship, but he wouldn't even if he could. Cynthia made his life better in every aspect. He would have been a fool to want otherwise. He wouldn't change a second of the time they'd spent together, and he sure as hell planned to devote more in the coming months, provided that she would spare them this hurdle.

It had all started with an impromptu after-hours meeting where things had gone from professional to personal before either one of them had realized the direction their conversation had taken off track. One thing had led to another until they'd both decided to continue their discussion within his hotel room in each other's arms.

"I don't want to do this here." Gareth kept his tone low, but he stopped her from exiting the foyer out to the connecting hallway. The elevator bank was right outside the glass entrance. "Let's take this either back to my hotel or your apartment."

"Gareth, you lost that type of privilege the moment I read

Brad's personnel file." Cynthia pulled her arm away from his grasp, spinning around so that she was mere inches from him. Her aggressive stance took him by surprise, especially considering Marilyn and anyone else who walked by could now overhear their private conversation. "I had one stipulation. One. And that was for you to never be untruthful with me."

"I didn't—"

"So help me if you stand there and tell me that a lie of omission isn't the same as lying…"

Okay, so she was one step past anger. Fury would better describe the words she'd managed to get through her clenched teeth, but at least it wasn't seething rage as far as he could tell. He'd count his blessings where he could find them.

"Fine. But I deserve a moment of your time to explain my discretion in this matter."

Gareth refused to back down from this, because she'd become too important to him to just walk away. Yes, he'd omitted certain facts about his past, but she sure as hell hadn't given him the opportunity to come clean with her, had she?

It was almost as if Cynthia had expected him to give up and walk out of this office as if their relationship had meant nothing to either of them. She stood resolutely in front of him, searching his gaze as if she expected him to abandon her.

"Lead the way, Cyn."

Gareth had fully intended his nickname for her to penetrate the barriers she'd solidified into place since he'd last seen her, right before Grace Dorrance had been arrested for murder. Whatever had taken place in that time had convinced her that they should no longer be together.

That conclusion was unacceptable to him.

She finally made her decision and guided them both down the carpeted hallway. Neither of them spoke again until the door to her office had been silently closed behind them. It didn't go amiss that she'd immediately placed the desk as a shield between them, although she remained standing so as not to give an inch of ground.

"Do you want to tell me what that phone call was about?" Gareth figured a great offense beat a good defensive every time. He stepped forward until the front of his legs were touching her desk. "I left your bed to catch a flight to Dubai with the promise of returning so that we could talk about our future, only to have you leave a voicemail telling me that we should take a break. That we should take a step back. It's not like you to run away without explaining why."

It was more than apparent by the way Cynthia inhaled sharply that she hadn't expected him to ignore the fact that he was Brad's biological brother. Good. They needed this cleared up before he shared such a personal aspect of his life anyway.

"I did no such thing," Cynthia countered, crossing her arms in a protective manner. She didn't like being on the defensive, but then again, neither did he. "In case you aren't up to speed, which I know for a fact that you spoke with Smith, Grace was arrested for Brad's murder. I was busy dealing with the fallout where one of my dear friends might be spending the rest of her life in prison for a crime she didn't commit, which all but proved to me that mixing business with pleasure was a mistake on our part."

Cynthia held up a hand when he would have disputed her findings, especially over a situation that had nothing to do with them.

"You seem to be forgetting that you threatened Brad's life the week before he was killed in cold blood. Do you even realize the position you put me in with my colleagues, friends, and even the police? Everyone in this office heard your threats, and they all knew the reason why—because Brad asked that I sever our relationship."

"And you know damn well that Brad Manon had no right to ask that of you." Gareth was getting sick and tired of having to keep his distance from her, but she still had her arms wrapped around herself. "Have you taken a good look at Grace and Rye Marshall? The man owns another firm that directly competes with Manon Investments. She handles all the damn trades, Cyn. You don't see a conflict of interest with that? I was a client long before you took the job as compliance officer. Brad's request had nothing to do with business and everything to do with me personally."

Fuck.

He'd walked right into that trap. That confession was exactly the one she'd wanted to hear.

Cynthia's arms dropped to her sides before she leaned forward to make sure she drilled home the point she was about to make.

"I couldn't have known that though, because you didn't see fit to tell me that you were Brad's brother." Cynthia's tone had become hard and her blue eyes displayed nothing other than anger. He'd delayed too long in sharing his history with her, and now he was set to pay the price. Only she didn't know that he was damned good at bartering. "I know exactly where I stand, Gareth. There's no need for you to spell it out for me. What I don't understand is why you didn't share your connection to Brad with the police."

"What makes you think I haven't done so?"

Gareth didn't take any satisfaction when Cynthia blinked and drew back to her previous position. She observed him rather cautiously as he slowly made his way around the desk, entirely finished with having an obstacle between them. She'd been throwing up way too many barriers as it was. He didn't stop closing the remaining distance until the tips of her black high heels were touching his dress shoes.

"Let me get this straight," Cynthia said as she did her best to control the tremor in her voice. He'd heard it anyway, which gave him the confidence that she wasn't *washing* her hands of their relationship. "You were comfortable enough with Detective Nielsen to tell him your family history, and yet you couldn't do the same with the woman you've shared a bed with for the past eight months?"

Double fuck.

Her ability to set a trap was unlimited. When would he learn?

"I know it doesn't sound good when you put it like that, but isn't that the exact excuse you were looking for to end things between us? You needed an excuse and this personal bit of information is just what you were looking for." Gareth caught Cynthia's quick inhalation at his accusation, but she sure as hell didn't deny the claim. Her lashes lowered when he slowly reached out to cup her cheek. He needed her to really hear what he was about to say. "Before you were even aware of my connection to Brad, you left me a voicemail telling me that we should take a break. You knew I was thousands of miles away and that there wasn't a damn thing I could do about it until I came home."

"Unlike your reasoning, my actions were for your benefit," Cynthia whispered, purposefully stepping back so that she was out of his reach. Her anger was waning though, which was what he'd been waiting for ever since he'd walked into this office. He'd learned early on that she wasn't a woman to be messed with when she had an objective in mind. "You can't say the same, and now I know where I stand."

Gareth shouldn't have done it, but he instinctively reached

out and pulled her to him until there wasn't a bit of air between them. She knew where she stood with him? No, she didn't. Not even close.

"I think about you every second of every goddamn day," Gareth muttered, wrapping his fingers around the back of her neck in order to tilt her head just so in order to claim her lips. Heat instantly spread through his body as if she'd lit a match. This woman had no idea just how much she affected him, but as she'd just pointed out…that was his fault because he hadn't moved fast enough. "Where do you stand? Right in front of me, Cyn. Right in front of me."

Gareth kissed her as he'd dreamt about every night he'd been away from her side. It didn't surprise him that she gave as much as she took. Her sexual preferences matched his in their depth. It was their emotional hang-ups that held them from moving forward.

It was time to rewrite the course of history.

He slowly ended their kiss, sensing the exact second she was no longer caught up in the moment. She rested her palms on the front of his suit jacket as she struggled for air and tensed her shoulders. He spoke before she could shut him down.

"My name is Gareth Nicollet. I was adopted into a wonderful family as an infant and only later got to know my birth mother. It's not something I can easily talk about, especially with a woman who's set such critical and exacting boundaries in our relationship." Gareth didn't give Cynthia the space she obviously wanted, opting to stay where he was directly in front of her. He didn't want to miss a single expression flash in those baby blues of hers. "I'm willing to shift some of those boundaries, Cyn. Are you prepared to do the same?"

CHAPTER THREE

"CYNTHIA, I WAS told that you needed to see me?" Paul had knocked, but he'd opened the door too quick for her to take a step back from Gareth. Honestly, she wasn't even sure an earthquake could have moved her from the place where her heels were glued to the plastic mat beneath her chair.

"Oh. Sorry. I didn't mean to interrupt." Paul's inquisitive gaze took in the scene before him. He was smart enough to know when to leave well enough alone. "You can catch up with me later. I'll be in my office."

And just like that, Cynthia was once again alone with Gareth. He was offering her the chance to hear his side of things, when she'd all but made up her mind to walk away.

It would have been the smart thing to do—to listen.

Still, she found herself delaying the inevitable.

Why did he have to be so drop dead gorgeous?

Gareth had a slight curl to his light brown hair that practically tempted a woman to run her hands through his thick mane. He had a lean body with cords of muscles that she could easily appreciate…and had explored that very course of action on more than one occasion.

Okay, many occurrences, to be honest.

And she hadn't harbored a single regret until yesterday.

"Did you really tell the police that you were related to Brad?"

Cynthia asked Gareth, searching his gaze for any shred of deceit.

"Yes."

Gareth's response was simple and said with no hesitation. Her wounded heart beat hard against her chest as she made a decision that was sure to bring more pain.

He'd misled her.

Yet she still had so many questions.

"I wasn't just some random woman you were involved with, Gareth," Cynthia said with incredulity, finding the strength to walk around him. She needed space to breathe. The pressure in her chest was becoming too much. She didn't turn around until she was able to hold onto the back of one of the guest chairs. "I worked for your brother for years. Do you know how foolish you made me look by keeping me in the dark? That's something I should have been privy to as someone you held close. It wasn't right that you kept secrets from me."

"In hindsight, you're right." Gareth held up his hands in forfeit, though she didn't believe for a second that he would ever admit defeat. "But no one other than Paul Slater and the compliance officer before you knew of my connection to Brad. That was just business, but you and I can discuss this tonight. I'd like to ask *you* something, though. Are you ever going to share with me why it is you believe every man who shares your bed will eventually lie to you?"

Cynthia found it hard to breathe once more, so she dug her fingers into the fabric of the chair to give herself leverage. She fought back her first reaction, which was to tell him that he had no right to ask something so personal when he'd been the one to hold back something so vital to her professional career.

But she'd given him that right the moment she'd joined him in his bed.

The gold flecks in his brown eyes were practically glowing

while he waited for her decision to confess her reasoning as to why she'd held back in their relationship.

Is that what they had?

Or had their time together simply been a brief office affair?

He was unlike any man she'd ever met, and that was saying something. She wasn't the type of woman to sleep around with just anyone. On the contrary, she was very particular about who she allowed in her private life. But she was surrounded by men day in and day out, especially in her chosen field of finance. She considered herself a good judge of character, but she'd come to find that she wasn't quite herself in the presence of Gareth Nicollet.

He made her vulnerable in a way she hadn't been since…

"You've made your point, but my past wouldn't have gotten you fired."

Cynthia realized her mistake the moment he'd heard her statement. She absolutely hated being on the defense. It was time she took ahold of the reins.

"Don't you dare stand there in front of me and say that your relationship with Brad had no bearing on my position at Manon Investments, because you know damn well that would be a blatant lie." Cynthia had been reeling ever since she'd pulled out Brad's personnel file to update his information. She shouldn't have had to find out that the man she'd been sleeping with was related to her boss…the same one who'd been murdered three weeks ago. "You knew. If you have the balls to ask me about the man who came before you, then you know how important honesty is to me."

Gareth didn't have a chance to respond to her accusations. It might have very well been for the best, because her emotions were starting to get the best of her. And if there was one thing she'd learned in her time at Manon Investments as their compliance officer, it was that she shouldn't let others see her sweat.

A light tap was heard on the door.

"Don't answer that," Gareth warned, taking a step forward in an attempt to stop her from answering whoever it was at the door. "We're not done."

"You once told me that you admired my work ethic, Gareth." Cynthia smoothed down the edges of her jacket after willing her fingers to let go of the chair. She needed a break before either one of them said something they'd later regret. If he were going to stay on as a client when Smith Gallo took over as portfolio manager, then she and Gareth would undoubtedly continue working together. "Or were you lying then, too?"

Okay.

That was unfair.

As a matter of fact, that was downright bitchy.

Cynthia didn't wait for his reply, because she didn't want to hear it. Honestly, she was afraid she'd cave under any excuse she was willing to latch onto.

Yes, she'd been the one who'd called him while he was out of the country to tell him that they should take a break. She'd done so before she'd ever found out that he'd lied regarding his relationship with Brad. There had been a damned good reason for her decision.

She was falling for him with all her heart and soul.

Who was she kidding?

She'd already fallen for him and desperately needed time to come to terms with what that meant for her future.

"That was pretty far below the belt, Cyn. Even for you."

It was, but he wasn't going to get an apology from her now.

She was in her early thirties. She'd been set in her ways by the time she was twenty-three. Space was essential to her mental wellbeing, and she needed it now more than ever.

Unfortunately, the woman standing on the threshold of her office told Cynthia that she wasn't likely to get it.

"Meredith." Cynthia wanted more than anything to turn around to witness Gareth's reaction to his sister-in-law. This visit was a total surprise, and there was an unspoken rule when it came to two self-assured women—never turn your back on the other. Self-preservation won out over curiosity. "What can I do for you?"

Numerous questions ran through Cynthia's mind.

What was Brad's ex-wife doing in the office? Why had she sought out Cynthia specifically, and where was Marilyn? She was the company's watchdog, and yet Cynthia had been caught unaware by an unannounced visitor.

Cynthia didn't miss the way the Meredith's gaze drifted past the door to Gareth.

"Gareth. It's been some time." Meredith seemed to wait for him to say something in return, but the tense silence stretched out until even Cynthia couldn't take it anymore. She purposefully shifted so that she was able to cut off Meredith's view of Gareth. "Cynthia, I was hoping I could speak with you in private."

There was absolutely no reason for Meredith to come to Cynthia for any reason.

"Meredith, can it wait?" Gareth asked, stepping in and attempting to take over. He might very well be used to getting his way in his own life, but this was Cynthia's office. He had no say in who or how she conducted her business. Besides, she needed some type of win today or else she'd be crawling to Laurel's office begging for that hidden bottle of wine her friend had stashed in her credenza. "We're—"

"Just finishing up," Cynthia smoothly replied for Gareth, deciding a moment away from him wasn't such a bad idea. He made her want things that weren't necessarily hers for the taking. "Gareth, I'm sure you can find your way out."

Cynthia tensed when those gold flecks in his eyes started radiating once more. He had a tendency to be unpredictable when that happened, but she slowly breathed a sigh of relief when he slowly nodded his acceptance of her decision.

Her relief was short-lived, however, when he took a small step toward her and whispered temptation in her ear.

"Tonight. My usual suite."

The message he sent with his profound stare when he pulled back told her that she'd better come prepared. She wasn't sure she was ready to bare her soul any more than necessary, especially considering the wound already administered by his knife.

Gareth didn't wait for a reply. Meredith stepped to the side and gave him the ability to cross the threshold and walk confidently away, leaving behind the faint scent of his cologne.

Why did she have a sudden urge to call him back?

"I didn't mean to interrupt," Meredith said sincerely, finally joining Cynthia in her office.

She was still at a loss as to what her boss' ex-wife could want to discuss that hadn't already been covered by Human Resources.

"It's fine." Cynthia managed to smile before closing the door. It didn't surprise her that Meredith didn't take a seat, but Cynthia was still reeling from the confrontation with Gareth. She walked around to her side of the desk and gratefully sank into the comforting leather of her desk chair. "Although I'm not sure I can help you. Paul mentioned the other day that you wanted to sell Brad's personal shares back to Manon Investments. That's perfectly legal and you're within your right to do so."

"Actually, I stopped by because of this," Meredith said with a bit of hesitation before pulling an envelope out of her purse. "I was going through Brad's belongings when I came across a letter he'd received from a man by the name of Kurt Langston."

Cynthia hadn't thought her day could get any worse. Wasn't it Laurel who was always going on about karma? This was all her fault. Cynthia had done a fine job of staying out of karma's way, but it appeared that a collision was unavoidable.

Nausea came in waves and it took every ounce of strength Cynthia had not to bend over her wastebasket. It was damned good thing she hadn't taken a drink of that smoothie she'd left on Laurel's desk.

"I'm confused as to why you would come to me with this." Cynthia's hands were no longer cold—they were completely numb. She'd lost feeling in her fingers altogether, and she didn't even bother to take the envelope from Meredith's grasp. All Cynthia could hope for was that the letter had to do with a compliance issue and that her name wasn't mentioned in the body of its contents. "From my understanding, Kurt Langston is the CEO of a technology company located here in Minneapolis."

Cynthia tried to maintain hope that Brad had invested some of his personal money into the tech company, though it was doubtful considering that he'd been in debt to the point that his financial position had been a focal point for the police early on in the murder investigation.

She still had faith that it wouldn't be about the one thing she'd tried the last three years to forget. The right decision had been made for all involved…by her. The only regret she had was that she'd been naïve enough to believe in fairy tales.

And then Gareth Nicollet entered the picture.

He made her want to believe that this wasn't the lesson she'd been supposed to learn. He made her want that elusive fairy tale of happily ever after.

Karma *was* a bitch.

"I'm sorry to tell you this, but Kurt Langston's letter had nothing to do with business. At least, as far as I could tell." Meredith leaned forward and gently laid the envelope directly in front of Cynthia. "This is just a copy. It was dated three years ago, but I felt compelled to give the original to the police. Did Brad or you have dirt on Kurt Langston? Could he have been the man responsible for Brad's death?"

CHAPTER FOUR

GARETH STARED OUT the living room window of the Executive WOW Suite at the W Minneapolis – The Foshay. The city lights had illuminated the streets below a few hours ago, and as always, the crowds had begun to invade the restaurants and bars to get a head start on their weekend. The chaotic scene below was his usual reminder that life's forward momentum was unavoidable regardless of one's own stumbling blocks.

"I had an affair with Kurt Langston."

He'd heard the lock of the hotel door activate, so he wasn't taken by complete surprise when Cynthia had spoken behind him. They'd both gotten used to the practice of him leaving a key at the front desk for her, although he'd recently been contemplating renting an apartment downtown for convenience sake. That would certainly make it easier to pack for these quick trips. Ever since meeting her, Minneapolis had come to be his second home.

He was certain that nothing she said in the next few minutes would change his mind.

"Did you hear me?"

"Yes." Gareth had shed his suit jacket a while ago, favoring a more comfortable ensemble of a loosened tie and rolled up sleeves. He tilted the glass in his hand, swallowing the rest of the smooth cool blended LaSalle whiskey he'd poured himself over a few cubes not five minutes ago. Even he could detect hints of dried fruits and honey. It was balanced against the spicy notes of Canadian rye with a round finish of raisins, cocoa, and brown sugar. He wasn't much of a drinker, but he was certain that he needed a quality rare whiskey to take the edge off of what he suspected was about to transpire. "I heard exactly what you said."

Gareth shifted his gaze up from the colorful display below to the image of the woman who had captured his heart eight months ago. Her reflection was stunning, but it didn't hold a candle to her form in the flesh.

"And?"

Cynthia had set her purse on the couch, tossing the cardkey along with it. There was an expectation in her tone that told him this wasn't their average benign conversation. She obviously believed that he was going to cast aspersions on her character for getting involved with a married man.

As a matter of fact, it seemed that she expected it.

How Gareth handled the next two minutes would set the foundation for their future relationship.

He finally turned around so that he could see every single emotion flash in those baby blues. Having the ability to gauge his opponent had been essential to his success.

This?

This woman standing before him was more about success than doubt. She had burrowed her way into his heart and had become a part of him that he could not deny himself. She'd somehow fused her soul with his in the short time they'd spent together.

And he didn't mind in the least.

She was his addiction.

"Your past liaisons have no bearing on our relationship, nor your reputation."

"Don't be obtuse," Cynthia snapped, taking a step forward on a pair of high heels without so much as a quaver. He'd never seen her wear them before, but the classic style suited her confident disposition. Right now, she was going on the offensive. She'd already made up her mind on how this confrontation was going to end. "Kurt Langston is married, and I had an affair with him. And yes, it matters."

Gareth had never met Langston, which was odd considering they had probably run in the same circles on more than one occasion. Either way, it was for the best the two men never came in contact with one another, because Gareth had no doubt that it would have ended in bloodshed now that he was aware of certain pertinent facts.

Smith had given Gareth a courtesy call regarding Meredith's recent visit to Cynthia this morning. To say his relationship with his sister-in-law was somewhat strained was an understatement. Technically, ex sister-in-law. He hadn't thought it was a good idea to stay around when he and Cynthia hadn't resolved matters concerning his familial connection with the Manons.

That didn't mean he wasn't worried about the reason Meredith had paid a visit to Cynthia. To find out that it concerned a past association that Cynthia had with Langston over three years ago took him by surprise at first.

"Are you still sleeping with him?"

Gareth knew damn well she wasn't still involved with the asshole, but it was clear that she needed to witness his unwavering support. He'd give her whatever the hell she needed, because he refused to watch her capitulate to a man who literally had no moral ethics.

"No, but that's not—"

"What matters?" Gareth began to walk toward her, taking

time to set his empty glass of melting ice on the coffee table. He absolutely refused to allow a man of so little worth to strip Cynthia of hers. He stopped a foot from where she stood, her perfect posture giving away the fact that she'd steeled herself for his verdict. "It certainly does matter, Cyn. You just said so yourself. You practically have the scruples of a saint. You hold others accountable to relatively the same degree, so I can without a doubt stand in front of you firmly trusting that you had no idea Langston was married when you became involved with him three years ago."

Cynthia's quick inhalation was followed by noticeable relief when she slowly released the air from her lungs. He should be downright pissed that she thought so little of him that she expected his reaction to be one of revulsion. He had kept in mind that he, himself, hadn't been completely honest with her. That alone would be hypocritical of him to make that kind of judgmental assessment.

"I can even guess how the end played out," Gareth continued, slipping his hands in his pockets to prevent himself from touching her. "You discovered he was married, you walked away, and his ego took a massive blow from which he had great difficulty recovering."

"A massive hit doesn't begin to cover it." Cynthia searched his gaze, though he wasn't sure what she was looking for after he'd clearly spelled out his stance on the subject. She then surprised him when she slipped her hands through his arms until she was able to lay her cheek against his dress shirt. Her heat immediately soaked into his. "Can we just take a moment?"

Gareth slowly pulled his hands from his pockets and wrapped her in a tight embrace.

He inhaled her intoxicating fragrance as he pressed a gentle kiss to the top of her head. Honestly, this was the first time he'd allowed himself to truly breathe. He'd been on edge ever since receiving her voicemail in Dubai.

They still had a lot of ground to cover, but he was grateful she'd lowered some of her barriers. She was a complex woman on a lot of levels. She made his life interesting in so many ways, from their in-depth conversations to her ability to keep up with him in a race. Their morning jogs when he was in town always invigorated him, especially when she would push herself to the finish line as if they were in a race for their lives.

How many times had they stayed up until two o'clock in the morning arguing politics, religion, or business? They'd even ventured into personal territory, but both of them had their reasons for being cautious in that particular area. It was time to go outside their comfort zone.

"What did the letter say that Langston wrote to Brad? Why would he involve your boss?"

"You've spoken with Smith, haven't you?"

"Possibly," Gareth countered with a half-smile, not wanting to throw Smith under the bus. The man had enough aggressive matters being hurled his way as he navigated a path for his new firm. "Is there anything I can do?"

Cynthia sighed as she stepped to the side, all but forcing Gareth to drop his arms. The imprint of her heat remained with him as she walked over to the small bar. This wasn't the average hotel room with a mini refrigerator posing as a minibar. The fully stocked shelves contained one of her favorite bottles of red wine, though he'd put in that request long ago. The label was now kept on hand, as well as his preferred Crown Royal XR.

"It appears that Kurt has found himself the center of attention recently." Cynthia poured herself a glass of the merlot from the bottle he'd let breathe for the last half hour. Some routines were rather soothing. "It wouldn't surprise me to find that our past relationship makes the morning headlines."

Smith's call had informed Gareth of the fact that Meredith had gone to the police with the letter Langston wrote. A threat was a threat, no matter how many years ago. It did beg the question, though—why involve Brad at all?

"I would think that is Langston's problem." Gareth joined her over at the bar, having grabbed his own rocks glass along the way. He began swirling the cubes. She was already holding the decanter up, anticipating his desire to join her in their traditional evening routine after she'd finished her workday. "You haven't spoken to the ass in three years?"

Cynthia couldn't hide her smile—the first one he'd seen since arriving back in the country—as she set the top of the crystal container back in its place. She picked up her wine and took a healthy sip. She closed her eyes to relish the taste, reminding him of other wayward moments. Now wasn't the time to partake in those thoughts.

"How do you know I haven't spoken to Kurt in three years?"

"I know," Gareth replied with confidence and a wink. He walked over to the couch, removing her purse from the cushion so that they'd have room to relax. "As a matter of fact, I'm surprised you didn't put the man in a hospital back then."

"I thought about it, but I ultimately decided he wasn't worth the time or effort."

Gareth didn't doubt that she'd considered physically assaulting the man who'd lied to her in such a fashion. But it was more in her nature to allow karma to handle such matters.

"So, is this where we share each other's sordid sexual history?"

Gareth had waited for Cynthia to join him, who kicked off her heels in her usual manner. He held up an arm, waiting for her to slip her bare feet onto his lap.

He didn't fool himself into thinking that this conversation wouldn't turn on him and his own history. He'd known from the moment he met her that she had issues with trust, and now he understood the reason why. The thing of it was, he didn't mind opening up to her after having made a decision that this was it.

As in…she was the *one*.

"Sordid pretty much sums it up, doesn't it?" Cynthia said rather reluctantly, though she propped a pillow up against the arm of the chair and rested her back against the additional support. She wiggled her toes and stared at her manicured nails polished in the shade of her lipstick. "I was naïve."

"Everyone's a sucker a time or two in their lives." It was the reason Gareth had invested money in Brad's firm to begin with, though it wasn't the reason he ended up keeping a percentage of his money in the hedge fund. "My mother tells me all the time that it's our bad experiences that shape us into a better person."

"Your mother?"

"You know, the woman who raised me," Gareth clarified with a fond smile, not wanting Cynthia to get off topic. He'd already made the decision to share his childhood with her. There was no going back, but they had a pressing issue with Langston if he was going to be an immediate problem. "It's aggravating as hell, but she's always right."

Cynthia hardly ever varied from the path in front of her, but he could easily sense that she'd jump the tracks if it meant she didn't have to give Langston another thought. Unfortunately, if her relationship with the asshole was going to be front and center in tomorrow's headlines in connection with Brad Manon's murder…well, it needed to be addressed before they became too distracted.

Gareth kneaded his fingers into the arch of her foot to soften the blow.

"Cynthia, tell me what happened. How did you become involved with a man like Langston?"

CHAPTER FIVE

CYNTHIA HAD SPENT the entire day going back and forth over a myriad of emotions. She'd been angry at Gareth for keeping information from her that was vitally important—not only to her career, but most importantly to their relationship. Then Meredith had walked in, bringing along with her a past that Cynthia would rather forget ever happened.

Forget was rather a loose word.

She'd wanted the past to stay dead and buried, six feet under. Make that twenty, for good measure. As a matter of fact, she wanted it cremated and the ashes to be scattered somewhere over Lake Superior that banished it forever to nowhere.

If there was one thing she hated more than the wrong shade of lipstick, it was being made a fool of by someone undeserving—a lowly peon.

"I met Kurt in a restaurant's lounge after having had dinner with Brad and Paul regarding Vern's seat on the board of directors. They weren't taking my advice on the fact that Phil Colbert should be the one to have that seat. He had more experience and had proven his worth to the firm ten times over."

Gareth had heard a lot about office politics regarding Manon Investments from her, so this bit of news wasn't anything new to him. Like with any business, things changed upon the flip of a coin…or so it seemed.

One of Cynthia's best friends had come into her own, earning a seat at the table. Laurel one hundred percent deserved the partnership spot that was up for grabs.

As for Smith Gallo, that man wasn't meant to have a seat on any table. It was written in his DNA not only to be one of the players, but to own the table and deal the seats out to the true power brokers of his own business.

"Anyway, Kurt was at the bar and offered to buy me a drink." Cynthia took a sip of her wine to wash away the distaste of those painful memories. She doubted that the entire bottle could achieve that success tonight. "He was charming, every bit a gentleman at that moment, and had the ability to make a woman not want to look past the façade. I fell for it hook, line, and sinker. Hell, I was nothing but a mind-numbed minnow by the time he got done dangling a weekend in Paris."

The thing of it was, Cynthia truly didn't care about material items. Sure, she bought designer shoes and handbags. Their workmanship was superior. She was a sucker for Prada, but even more so Jimmy Choo. She certainly didn't mind paying for quality over quantity.

Bottom line, she dressed for success with discerning taste.

That didn't mean she couldn't don a pair of faded blue jeans, topped off with a white cotton sleeveless t-shirt when the need arose. She worked the skin right off her fingers when she pitched in to help build houses for Habitat for Humanity.

Gareth had even convinced her to fly to Cambodia to help him scout for land in order to set up regional health clinics. He'd said at the time that her enthusiasm to help others was astounding to witness, but even more so enjoyable to observe when she'd gone into an orphanage to play with abandoned children who had nothing but her attention.

It was rare they ever ventured too much into their personal

goals in life, but he had mentioned that he'd love to adopt when he was finally ready for that phase of his life.

Her heart was still agonizing at where the still fresh wound was inflicted by the discovery that he hadn't been truthful about his past out of lack of trust.

Honestly, the only thing he'd told her about his childhood was that he was from a family who'd made it their mission to help others with their less than modest wealth. The family's trust funds had more cash in the accounts than the next five generations could spend in their lifetimes. It was the reason he'd obtained a master's degree in humanities. He wanted to continue the tradition of his family by helping others—helping people to help themselves through hospitals and schools.

"When did you find out he was married?"

"There was a small article written in the society pages about a local tech company that was about to explode. Imagine my surprise to read that Kurt Langston had the most supportive wife when it came to that endeavor. I never thought the expression *seeing red* was literal until that very moment."

Cynthia set her wineglass on the coffee table, giving herself the ability to remove her suit jacket. The confines of the material were too tight given the lack of any moving air, and she needed a bit of breathing room. She still had on a white silk blouse that was complemented by a string of pearls. It was by far his favorite piece of jewelry she owned, though that most likely had to do with the fact that he'd made love to her while that was the only object on her body.

It was also the reason she wore her pearls every time he was town. There was nothing wrong with a bit of mischievous behavior now and then.

"I confronted Kurt that same night, though he'd been expecting my reaction because of the article." Cynthia settled back against the pillow with her wineglass in hand. Gareth had stopped kneading her arches and was lightly stroking the soft skin of her calves. It dawned on her that Kurt had never taken the time to sit with her like this when they could spare a few minutes together. She supposed it wasn't that much of a shock to learn that Kurt was nothing but a conniving scumbag with money. He never really made much of an effort to disguise that fact. She'd just been blind. "He quickly turned the tables and all but threatened me if I so much as breathed a word of our affair to anyone in our mutual social circles. You see, we'd both agreed at the start to keep our relationship quiet for various other reasons, but it turned out that the key reason was because of a marriage I hadn't known existed."

"And Brad's connection to Langston? I'm having trouble understanding why Langston would provide evidence of such an affair in a letter to your boss."

Gareth hadn't touched a drop of his second drink. She had a rising suspicion that he might need a clear head in case he needed to make some urgent phone calls to clear up this unfortunate problem. His altruistic lifestyle might make an unscrupulous person believe he was a mark, but he was anything but in matters that concerned his family and the handling of their humanitarian pursuits.

She certainly didn't fit in that specific category, but something told her that he'd go the extra mile for her. It was the sole reason she hadn't left him another voicemail that she was cutting all ties. She couldn't bring herself to cut the cord that bound them.

Gareth had cut his business trip short, proving to her that he wasn't giving up on what they'd built over the course of eight months. Granted, she'd tried to do the right thing by walking away in the first place. Everyone had become a bullseye in this game of office roulette. She hadn't wanted Gareth or herself to become the next victim of the unknown killer.

"I know. It doesn't make any sense," Cynthia said with a shake of her head. She barely suppressed a groan of pleasure when Gareth began once again to knead the arch of her foot. There was something so damned sexy about a man who knew how to use his hands in the right way. "Don't get me wrong. Kurt didn't come right out and confess that we'd had an affair in the letter, though I could see why Meredith would believe there was a connection between us. His words indicated that he would sue should any employee of Manon Investments smear his name for any reason."

"That tells me that Brad already knew of your affair with Langston." Gareth was obviously assuming the same thing she was regarding the letter. Something wasn't adding up, but it wasn't like Brad was around for them to ask questions. "Did you let it slip to Brad that you had been seeing Langston?"

"No, not at all." Cynthia answered with absolute conviction. "My name was included in the letter, but more so as the compliance officer who had a job to do, which is why Meredith brought me the letter. She had no idea that I'd had been a victim of an affair with Kurt."

"Does Meredith know now?"

"Absolutely." Cynthia met his gaze. She wanted to gauge his reaction to her reply, but it wasn't like he'd cast any stones. Her confession hadn't had him running in the other direction. "I didn't see a point in hiding it if I was going to come clean with the police. She needed to know that I had nothing to do with this matter."

Cynthia had called Detective Nielsen right after Meredith left the office. He'd been the detective who'd questioned Gareth about his empty threat to kill Brad. His words had been taken out of context, presumably by Marilyn.

Definitely by Marilyn.

Truthfully, it wouldn't surprise Cynthia in the least if Marilyn knew exactly who killed Brad Manon. The woman was a wealth of information, both public and private, but wasn't there always one of those individuals in every office?

"Which is why you believe that Langston will be front page news tomorrow."

"Most certainly. A juicy tidbit like that? You know someone down at the station will leak Kurt Langston's involvement to the press. It only makes sense." Cynthia bit her bottom lip as she imagined the chaos that would erupt over the news. It wasn't her intention to hurt Kurt's wife. "What if I'm wrong, though? What if whatever clandestine clash that was going on between Brad and Kurt had nothing to do with me?"

Then an innocent woman would end up being hurt by some extramarital affair that happened three years ago.

Cynthia had struggled a lot back then on whether or not to reach out to Jane Langston. The woman had no idea what her husband did in his spare time. She didn't deserve to be married to a man who had so little respect for her, but some quaint social nicety had stopped Cynthia from making contact with Kurt's wife—and her reservations had nothing to do with Kurt's threat.

Had Cynthia only been wanting to ease her own conscience? If so, that wouldn't have been fair to Jane Langston. Cynthia would have appeared to be a bitch who'd set out to catch a married man, regardless that the assumption was furthest from the truth, and Kurt would have somehow come out smelling like roses.

Looking back, it was clear that she hadn't done anything wrong. That didn't absolve her of the guilt she felt for sleeping with a conniving asshole who'd purposefully misled her in their time together just to get into her panties.

"That's why we're going to leave the matter to the professionals. It's a police matter." Gareth's brown eyes began to flash those gold flecks, all but warning her that the outcome of any other decision could be very, very bad. He must have heard in more detail what Grace and Rye had gone through from Smith. "You did what you thought best, now it's time to leave well enough alone."

Cynthia cocked an eyebrow, but he wasn't about to be drawn into a debate over Kurt. She couldn't help but smile behind the rim of her glass. They still had a lot of ground to cover tonight, but she needed to take a minute after having bared her heart regarding a mistake that would have eaten at her soul for the rest of her life.

It was better that it was all out in the open.

"I'm serious, Cyn. Some homicidal psychopath saw fit to kill Brad Manon in cold blood. I wasn't here when Grace was caught in the killer's crosshairs, but I don't want you anywhere near that playing field. This individual is playing for keeps."

She wasn't going to argue with him, but that didn't mean she wouldn't take the time to grill Marilyn a little more than usual. What would be wrong with learning more about the employees she worked with five days out of the week? No one ever wanted to be friends with the compliance officer. That meant she had to use certain tactics to keep tabs on everyone's personal lifestyle that just might affect the business.

Cynthia took another sip of her wine, thinking about the two women who made her job just measurably bearable.

Laurel and Grace were the exception to the rule. It was Laurel who had connected the three of them during a social event, and neither one of them seemed to care that Cynthia was the overseer of all legal activities at the firm. The fact that Laurel had come strutting into the office with a bottle of merlot and announced that no one needed to know a thing about their aftermarket hours get-togethers had hit the nail on the head.

Cynthia's lashes began to close as Gareth continued to work his magic. He was now massaging her lower legs in a rhythm that had her sinking lower into the cushion. She eventually got rid of the pillow so that she could stretch out a little more.

It seemed to her that she could sense the moment Gareth was going to speak. She'd never been attuned to a man the way she was with him, and that included many more than Kurt Langston. In hindsight, all Kurt had done was distract her with adventure that she hadn't seen fit to provide for herself.

Cynthia supposed she should be thankful to him for one lesson, because he'd taught her that she hadn't needed a man to make her happy. She was proud of who she'd become, though she could admit to holding men to higher standards more often than they could meet.

It was unfortunate that Gareth had come immediately after her valuable lesson, when the sting was still fresh.

She'd always tended to act first and suffer the consequences later. It was in her genetic makeup to be out in front of any issue. She made decisions, in and out of her personal life, and stuck to them. Maybe it was time she give a little bit.

"We could always table this discussion until later," Cynthia managed to draw out around a moan he initiated by working on a knot in her right calf that had been bothering her all day.

She lifted the lashes on her right eye to witness his reaction. He hadn't even flinched at her confession. She could at least give him the benefit of the doubt about why he'd kept his relationship with Brad a secret.

She owed him that much, didn't she?

To prove that she wasn't just delaying the inevitable—which

she'd asked for—she raised a knee so that her foot rested against the growing bulge in his pants.

"Are you trying to distract me with sex, Cyn?"

"Is it working yet?"

CHAPTER SIX

G ARETH GENTLY REMOVED Cynthia's legs from his lap,
careful not to spill either of their drinks. He would have
certainly allowed her to continue to control the narrative had he
not known of her reaction this morning. It was easy to see that
the day's events weighed heavily on her mind.

She shouldn't have to carry any more emotional baggage
than was necessary, especially when he was the one who could
ease her burdens.

"You could tempt a saint, Cyn." He meant every word of
that statement, too. "And I'm about as far away from sainthood
as I could possibly get."

Gareth managed to stand, though it was rather uncomfortable to move positions at the moment. He decided not to waste
the drink in his hand. The smooth whiskey was probably the
only thing that could take the edge off his current condition.

"I didn't know I was adopted until the age of six." Gareth
heard her shift on the couch, but he didn't bother to turn around
yet. Instead, he walked over to the large windowpane that
overlooked the city. "The thing of it was, I don't believe Mom or
Dad kept that fact from me on purpose. They loved me as if I
were their biological child. There was no distinction between me
and my brothers and sisters."

Gareth waited for Cynthia to ask questions. He was used to
telling this story, though it was usually to the children left behind

in the orphanages. His story was vastly different from a dear friend who'd had the opposite experience. Together, they balanced one another in their sentiments about the children's futures. Those left behind deserved the unvarnished truth.

"Gareth." The way Cynthia said his name told him that she wasn't going to give him the usual reaction. It didn't surprise him, really, though this was the exact conversation she'd wanted to have this morning. He met her gaze in the reflection of the windowpane. "You're pretty damn close to sainthood, from where I'm standing."

"You weren't saying that this morning," Gareth replied wryly, lifting the rocks glass to his lips. He drained half the contents in one swig. "And the very public act of giving my family's money back to the community doesn't qualify, because there are other things I do in the shadowy interim that could have possibly blackened my soul."

Cynthia's laughter rang out and rebounded off the periphery of the living room, though he couldn't understand why she found his sentiment so damn funny. It was the plain truth, whether she wanted to recognize it for what it was or not.

"You find that amusing?"

"It's a long story, but I'll save you a warm seat in hell. Laurel and Grace have promised to join me, so we'll just throw one big bash." Cynthia had been leaning over the arm of the couch, but she unfolded her slender frame before setting her wineglass back down on the side table. She'd balanced the delicate stem between her fingers as she landed the glass on the stone surface with a purpose. She glided across the room, giving him the pleasure of viewing the sensual sway of her hips. His eyes might be trained elsewhere, but he didn't miss the slow fade of her beautiful smile. "We've both sinned, Gareth. We're human. And I realized after today that my expectations were set a bit higher than even most saints could meet. I expected nothing short of perfection from you, and that wasn't quite fair. But neither one of us are going anywhere at the moment. There's plenty of time to talk, but what I truly need right now is you."

Cynthia was now standing directly behind him. She quietly rested her hands on his shoulders before stepping even closer, crushing the heat that was simmering between their bodies. The alcohol he'd consumed was no match for her intoxicating mixture of scent and touch.

"I like this spot," Cynthia whispered encouragingly, pulling down his shirt collar so that she could press her lips to the back of his neck. "I can do this small gesture so simple and sweet, yet still enjoy the vastness of the view before us."

Cynthia gradually reached around him and began to unfasten the buttons on his shirt one by one. She was peering over his shoulder and observing her handiwork, especially when she finished tugging the trapped fabric from his dress pants.

"We might be on a floor of this hotel high enough so that no one can see what we're doing, but that doesn't mean someone hasn't gone the extra mile and invested in a pair of binoculars or a gold-plated telescope designed for this specific purpose."

Gareth switched the glass of whiskey to his other hand as she pulled the material down his arms. She didn't stop there, pulling his sleeveless undershirt up and over his head. He did love her determination.

"Well, we wouldn't want to disappoint someone who's gone that extra mile, now would we?" Cynthia trailed one of her manicured nails across his back as she began to walk around him. She took her time admiring his frame until she was standing directly in front of him. "Unless a little exhibitionism makes you uncomfortable?"

Gareth drained the rest of his whiskey to prevent himself

from reacting to her taunt.

She wanted to play?

He sure as hell wasn't about to say no to that.

"Just remember, Cyn, it goes both ways."

Gareth had to remind himself to follow through with his promise, but it was rather hard to concentrate when she gracefully lowered herself to her knees. The stimulating reflection in the window had his cock hardening in anticipation.

"I expected nothing less," Cynthia said provocatively, un-hooking his belt before slipping the small black onyx oval through the buttonhole.

Any reply Gareth would have made was stopped when she withdrew his throbbing member from its confines. Damn if he couldn't have come right then and there. He widened his stance to give himself better leverage.

It was a good thing he'd locked his knees. The arousing sensation of her tongue flicking against his tip was nearly enough to have made him collapse and join her on the floor.

He tightened his grip on the empty glass, wishing he hadn't finished its contents quite so quickly.

The red brake lights and the illuminating headlights on the vehicles below continued to pass one another in an array of colorful streaks. Under normal circumstances, he would have been happy to observe the world carry on at a rapid pace below. Nothing was as captivating as witnessing Cynthia take him in her mouth before slowly setting up a rhythm where the edges of her black hair moved against her jawline in time with her rhythmic movements.

"Don't—"

Gareth's words became strangled when she did the exact thing he'd intended to warn her against. She'd taken his cock to the back of her throat and swallowed. The tight constriction around his tip was beyond intense. He instinctively used his free hand and threaded his fingers through her silky strands.

"Hmmmm."

Cynthia no doubt hummed on purpose, allowing the vibrations of her voice travel down his shaft.

"Cyn. Pure sin."

His play on her name didn't escape her, but she didn't allow that to distract her from pleasuring him at her pace. She drew her head back, caressed the underside of his cock with her tongue, and sucked him back into her mouth until his tip hit the back of her throat.

Once again, he tightened his hold on her hair in warning. She ignored his attempt to control the situation by using her hands to pull him forward. His sac began to tighten in its natural bid to release its contents.

It was clear that she wanted to finish him off in this manner, but she was denying them both the prolonged pleasure of what lay before them this evening.

"Cyn, that's enough."

Her answer was to quicken the pace and accent the rhythm that she'd set. Gareth wasn't kidding himself, because he could have easily prevented her from continuing just from his hold of her hair. He would have to adjust his stance accordingly. The influence she had over him was too much to resist.

Cyn quickened the cadence at which her lips and tongue glided over his cock, but it was when she suddenly stopped that her exploit triggered his release. She was very gifted with her tongue and managed to stroke just the right area that had her name flying off his lips.

"Do you think whoever invested in that telescope got their money's worth?"

"If they hadn't before, they sure have now," Gareth muttered before helping her stand. Her arched eyebrow all but dared him to spin her around so that she was facing the window. "Hold this. And whatever you do, don't drop it."

Gareth had given her his empty glass, allowing him free rein to unfasten the small buttons on her silk blouse. The action allowed him the ability to come down off the high she'd initiated. By the time he'd uncovered her white lace bra, he was somewhat in control of his breathing.

"There's something wickedly delicious about you wearing white lingerie." Gareth began to hike her penciled skirt, though that wasn't an easy endeavor. He managed to get the taut material up and around her hips, giving him the distinct pleasure of seeing her matching delicate panties. "So angelic and pure, yet so enticingly sinful."

Gareth met her gaze in the reflection of the window.

"Lift your arms, Cyn." She did as he instructed, though he didn't doubt this was exactly how she wanted things to go. "And remember, don't drop the cut crystal."

Cynthia had bent her arms at her elbows, almost as if she were embracing him. He lowered his eyes to her bare feet. Her smile in the reflection told him that she was very much going to enjoy this next part.

What she didn't know was that he wasn't going to let her off that easy.

"Gareth, what makes you think you could make me drop this hunk of glass?"

CHAPTER SEVEN

CYNTHIA SUCKED IN a breath when Gareth slid his fingers under the waistband of her lace panties. His fixed gaze at her eyes' opaque reflection in the windowpane never wavered from hers, which told her that he intended to watch every single expression of euphoria that crossed her features.

They both liked to play games in the bedroom, although relishing in each other's pleasure had never been done quite so publicly.

She wasn't worried at the off chance someone was watching.

They were too high up for the traffic below to make out what anyone was doing behind the glass panels. Yet his comment about binoculars and telescopes had certainly added an exciting edge of intrigue to their evening.

"You do like playing with fire, don't you?" Gareth murmured, wrapping an arm underneath her breast to pull her tighter against his chest. "Spread your legs, Cyn. Let's see who wins this duel."

She loved a challenge, but he always managed to up the ante by that last all in chip count.

"And if I win?"

Gareth barely grazed his middle finger over her clit, but it was enough to awaken every single nerve in her entire body. She didn't spread her legs for him as much in obedience as she did out of instinct. Her knees had almost buckled at the first simple caress. She didn't doubt there was more to come that would have her begging for her release.

"You won't," Gareth replied with total confidence. "You're soaked, Cyn. And we haven't even begun to explore your depths."

Gareth spread her juices over his fingers, slowly dipping into her. This time he traced around the very edges of her clit to draw out her pleasure to an exquisite yearning. She didn't doubt that he'd try to do his worst, but she had the advantage in this position. All she had to do was rock her hips away from his touch, but she couldn't quite manage to spoil all the fun as of yet.

The heat of his breath caressing her neck sent shivers of arousal down her spine. His body was solid as a rock wall against her supple skin. There was something inherently sexual about the strength of a man's taut physique.

The manner in which he was continually stroking the sides of her clit as if he was thrusting against her intensified her awareness.

"Don't close your eyes." Gareth's small directive somehow heightened her responsiveness even more. "I want to see your reaction when I make you come with just the slightest touch of my fingers."

Cynthia tried to lock her knees into place to prevent them from trembling, but he was now pressing on her sensitive nub while moving his fingers in centric circular motions.

When his other hand slipped under the lace of her bra and brushed her nipples, her grip on his glass marginally slipped an inch.

Laughter bubbled when she heard him chuckle, but she wasn't ready to give in quite yet.

"I was just testing you to see if you were paying attention,"

Cynthia said somewhat breathlessly, trying to gain back a bit of control. It was rather hard when he was steadfast in his endeavor to make her come. "You'll have to do more than touch my—"

Gareth lightly pinched her nipple to bring her up short.

"Better," Cynthia encourage, though the word sounded a bit strangled. A spasm of pleasure took hold the exact moment he slipped a finger inside of her. When he added another, it was then she realized that he was going to use the base of his hand to maintain pressure on her clit. With every slow thrust of his fingers, her clit was massaged simultaneously. "Hmmm, I see you're attacking on all fronts."

"You wouldn't have it any other way."

Every caress and stroke he gifted her with was nothing compared to the sight of him pleasuring her.

There they stood, two people in the throes of passion, basically on top of the world. Everyone else was going about their lives, but she and Gareth had blocked off everything and everyone to concentrate on each other.

They'd become one with the reflection in front of them.

The more moans he elicited from his touch, the darker his gaze became as he watched her come apart, giving him the ultimate gift—submission to his will.

Cynthia involuntarily cried out his name when the addition of a third finger had her sheath clamping down on his fingers. Her knees could no longer hold her upright, but she didn't need to worry about falling. He'd released her breast and was holding her body tightly against his chest.

She rode the waves of blissful indulgence until all she wanted to do was curl up in his embrace and recover for the next round.

There was always a next round with him.

"Gareth?" She'd laid her head back on his shoulder, so she didn't doubt that he'd heard her. To preface her next statement, she brought her left arm down so that he could witness her victory. "I win."

"I WAS AROUND twenty years old when I found out the name of my birth mother."

Cynthia opened her eyes upon Gareth's confession, his warmth surrounding her more so than the comforter he'd pulled over them sometime in the middle of the night. The morning sun was beginning to shine through the heavy drapes of the hotel's bedroom, but she'd heard somewhere that snow was in the forecast. Seeing as it was Saturday, there was no need to rush out of bed and into the office.

"Did you go and meet her?"

Their quiet tones maintained a semblance of intimacy. During the past eight months, they'd learned a lot about each other physically and mentally. She'd come to find that Gareth had a rather high IQ, but he was also wise beyond his years. He'd rubbed shoulders with every sort in his life's pursuit of understanding. Honestly, there were times his patience made her look like a teenage girl who was told she couldn't have the new model iPhone that all her evolutionally challenged friends already enjoyed.

Gareth claimed her ability to speak bluntly and make no apologies for her opinions was endearing. He did the same, though it was done with a lot more elegance. She tried her best now to give him the courtesy she hadn't yesterday.

"Yes." Gareth rested an arm over her hip, allowing her to snuggle deeper into his embrace. She wasn't able to witness his expressions, but she didn't need to. Emotion had thickened his voice. "I wasn't expecting her to have an older son. Usually, it's the other way around. From what she told me, she'd had Brad at a young age. It wasn't until later that she met a man who'd taken her for every penny she'd ever worked for, leaving her high and dry."

"And pregnant?"

"Yes. She went on to explain that she could barely make ends meet and that it was clearly impossible for her to raise two children." Gareth displayed no resentment. None. There was almost a sense of closure to his tone. "I don't begrudge her for making the obviously necessary decision. In hindsight, it was probably the best for everyone involved. She was able to give Brad Manon a secure foundation and raise him without the worry of added expenses, all the while knowing that I was being raised by a good, solidly grounded family."

"Did you meet Brad then?"

"Yes." Had she not been paying attention, she would have missed the slight tension in his bicep. "Honestly, he had no interest in me or who I was. Looking back, I believe that my presence brought up bad memories of a time that he would have rather forgotten entirely. I can't say I blame him. From what I'd heard, my biological father hadn't been the most upstanding man. He had been a player without any morals."

Cynthia thought back to those times when Gareth would visit the office to discuss his investment. Every one of those meetings had involved Paul. Had she known that Gareth and Brad were related, it would have been more than obvious that there was bad blood between the two. As it stood, Gareth had appeared to her as any other client.

"When did the two of you reconnect?"

"At his mother's funeral. It was somewhat apropos."

Cynthia no longer wanted to be staring at the dim rays of sunshine that faded every time a cloud passed overhead. He was sharing with her one of the most private moments of his life. He deserved her full attention.

She scooted forward a bit so that she could roll over, using the blankets as leverage. Once she was in position, she rested her cheek against the pillow so they were eye to eye.

His tender smile spoke volumes.

"Jenny and Todd Nicollet are my parents. They raised me, provided for me, and loved me as they do their own biological children." Gareth brushed away a strand of her black hair that had fallen on her cheek. "You'll have to come to one of our family gatherings. Grounded is an understatement in so many ways. My brothers and sisters can be a riot when we start competing for the family cornhole championship."

The smooth manner in which Gareth had brought up meeting his parents was not lost on her. She allowed him that small victory. It was a much-needed diversion for him to take a small break before diving into the barely discernable relationship he'd clearly had with his brother.

"It's good that you recognize healthy competition. My father is the reigning champ of the billiards table in our house. Actually, straight pool is his favorite, and he calls every shot."

Cynthia had taken a minor victory a time or two, but it was never for the title. They detoured a bit by talking about what sports they used to play, who held the titles of which activity, and made some side bets that would no doubt make for interesting stakes.

"What happened at the funeral?" Cynthia finally asked when they'd both fallen quiet. She stroked her foot over his calf so that he wouldn't feel so isolated on this short visit to the past. "Did Brad finally want a relationship of any kind?"

"You could say that." Gareth sighed in resignation. He propped himself up on his elbow, a low level of agitation entering his body. "He wanted access to part of my family's money. He was in the beginning phases of starting up the hedge fund. I obviously couldn't do that, because the trust funds are run by a rather prestigious accounting firm. And I wasn't going anywhere near the finances of the charity organizations we support with established endowments."

Cynthia wasn't the compliance officer at the firm's inception. She'd come on a couple of years later when their former employee decided to move to California for his wife's promotion to a recently established regional sales manager's position with Pfizer during a reorganization of territories. He'd done a fine enough job, but there were areas that he'd been lax. He wasn't exactly the family's breadwinner anymore. The choice had been a simple one to make, and he'd turned over his duties happily. All in all, the transition had been seamless.

It was due to her role in the company that she was well aware that the money Gareth had invested in Manon Investments was from his own personal income. Being on several corporate boards, dabbling in prime key real estate that was vulnerable after the bubble burst, and some very high-risk investments had turned him quite a hefty profit, which had continued to exponentially redouble his wealth in his young life thus far with unlimited potential.

"Brad was confident his new firm could make a name for itself. I offered to give a percentage of my portfolio to the hedge fund, and he happily took the investment." Gareth reached out, taking a lock of her hair and twisting it around his finger. It was evident he'd been taken to another place and time. "Only there was one unexceptional caveat."

It was then that the light bulb that had come close to shattering yesterday began to brighten.

"Brad didn't want anyone to know that the two of you were

related." Cynthia made the statement, but couldn't connect the dots just yet. "But why? One would think having you invest…"

Cynthia didn't finish her sentence, because it finally became clear why Brad had made such an incidental request. His pride had always been on the high side, but it hadn't become dark until a few years ago.

"Brad thought people inside the industry would view my investment as a handout versus me having faith in his abilities, so he asked me to keep our family affiliation quiet. I gave my word, Cyn."

"We kept our involvement quiet for the most part because of my position, but you and Brad had a rather heated exchange around three or four months into it. That argument was about our relationship, wasn't it?"

"Yes." Gareth gave her an endearing grin before smoothing her hair back in place. "I told him enough time had passed since the inception of the firm that no one would care about our family connection. He felt very differently. Look, we weren't close. I realized early on that he wanted nothing to do with me personally. The only reason he wanted even the slightest association had everything to do with my money. I should have pulled my investment long ago because of that, but he was damned good at turning a profit. It made good business sense to stay. So, we came to a mutually beneficial agreement."

Cynthia recalled the week before Brad was murdered. He'd marched into her office and all but demanded to know if she had been seeing Gareth. As of yet, she had no idea how he'd initially come to discover her relationship with his brother.

In her usual fashion, she wasn't in the least embarrassed about the time she'd spent with Gareth. Did it break any professional rules? No, but it certainly didn't look ethical for the firm's compliance office to be dating a client, even though she didn't have anything to do with his investment portfolio.

That entire confrontation led to Gareth discovering that Brad had demanded she end things, and now she—for the first time—understood the reason why. That didn't negate the fact that other employees had heard Gareth threatening to kill Brad…figuratively.

"Thank you," Cynthia whispered, raising up to press her lips against his. She wouldn't apologize for overreacting at first, per se. Anyone would have been angry to discover such a secret that could in adversely affect her career. "I appreciate your honesty, Gareth."

He pushed her back down, kissing her passionately and letting her know that he had no intention of letting her get out of bed anytime soon. It was a good thing it was Saturday. She had a feeling that she wouldn't set foot outside this hotel room for the next forty-eight hours.

It was also a good thing this lovely hotel had five-star room service.

"I would give my life before ever intentionally hurting you. If you didn't know it by now, Cyn, I love you very much."

CHAPTER EIGHT

GARETH WALKED INTO the offices of Manon Investments, soon to be Gallo Capital Management. It was going on seven-thirty in the morning, and the office was alive with busy people moving here and there on a mission. Minneapolis was on central time, which meant the market's opening would be taking place in just an hour from now. He wasn't surprised to see the majority of the staff getting ready for the day, the receptionist behind her desk, and the televisions already fired up in the trading room.

"Gareth, it's good to see you again," Laurel said, walking past him in the foyer with a smile and a cup of coffee in her hand. She'd obviously spoken to Cynthia this morning, although it had to have been after she'd left the hotel at five-thirty to head back to her place so that she could grab a clean outfit. "Will you be using the guest office today?"

"Yes. Actually, I'm hoping to use it for the rest of this week." Marilyn had taken notice of his arrival and was already out of her seat. "I don't fly out until Friday. Good morning, Marilyn."

Laurel continued to head in the direction of her office while Marilyn showed him to the guest office the firm set aside for visiting clients. She took in that he was carrying a cup of coffee from the downstairs café, along with a protein smoothie for Cynthia.

The weekend had gone by faster than either of them had wanted, but every minute had been uniquely treasured. They'd spent more time talking and getting to know one another than they had making love, which was a turn of events that each of them expressed their appreciation for earlier this morning. Who would have thought that they'd be laughing at four o'clock on a Sunday morning about the shapes of their mate's toes? She'd gone into a long explanation of why the right pedicure could make the ugliest feet look as if they should appear on a saddle commercial.

"Can I get you anything else, Mr. Nicollet?"

"No, thank you." Gareth set down the disposable tray holder he'd been carrying in his right hand on the desk before doing the same with his briefcase. "This will be fine. Has the guest password changed recently?"

"No, it's the same as before. Paul has a breakfast meeting, but he's due back to the office around ten o'clock. Would you like me to put you on his schedule?"

"Please. I'd appreciate that." Gareth had quite a few things to go over with Paul, but there was someone else he needed to speak with regarding his investments. That was one topic that he and Cynthia had avoided, but he completely understood her position on the matter. "Is Smith in this morning?"

"Yes, he arrived about an hour ago."

Gareth would have followed Marilyn out of the guest office, but she made no attempt to leave. As a matter of fact, her fingers were laced tightly in front of her as she stood at attention. She obviously wanted to speak with him, but she was waiting for his cue.

"Is there something else?" Gareth asked cautiously, having heard numerous rumors about almost every employee in the firm while talking with Cynthia this weekend.

His brother had been murdered in cold blood, the police investigation appeared to focus on the staff, and Cynthia's friends had reluctantly been drawn into the case for various different reasons.

He never should have flown to Dubai.

"I just want to express my condolences. I'm so, so sorry for the loss of your brother."

For a brief moment, Gareth wondered if he'd heard Marilyn incorrectly. He and Cynthia hadn't gotten the most quality of sleep this weekend, so it was possible that he'd misinterpreted the conversation.

"If there's anything else I can get you, please let me know."

Marilyn offered him a comforting smile and a nod before separating her hands to return to her desk.

"Marilyn, how exactly did you discover that Brad and I were related?" Gareth abruptly asked, not willing to let this matter slide. No one outside of Brad, Paul, and the previous compliance officer were aware of the familial connection. "I apologize if I'm coming across as being a bit too abrupt, but the relationship Brad and I had was rather…artificial."

"Oh, please don't think I told anyone," Marilyn said rather anxiously, appearing rather worried that she'd done something wrong. She was back to wringing her hands. It hadn't been Gareth's intention to upset her, but it was rather important to find out how she'd come to be aware of his connection to Brad. That kind of information could aid in the police investigation. "I was taking notes in a meeting that Paul had with Michael when the firm opened its doors. He realized his mistake immediately and swore me to secrecy. I promise you that I haven't said a word to anyone including the authorities, which is why I waited until I had a private moment with you before extending my condolences."

It made sense, but Paul should have come clean with Gareth about the fact that someone else was privy to his information. It did beg the question who else knew his private information.

"It's fine, Marilyn. I didn't mean for you—"

"Gareth, it's good to see you. I heard you were in town." Smith stood in the frame of the office doorway, cutting off Gareth's apology. The man was wearing one of his tailored suits and looking right at home in his newly acquired firm. This man might come from wealth, but he was one of the most dedicated, hardworking men in his profession. "I'm not sure what your schedule is for the day, but I'd love to sit down and talk to you about the future of our newly established fund."

Marilyn retreated back to her desk while the two men shook hands. Gareth made a mental note to ask her more questions sometime later today.

"I have a quick phone call to make, but then I'm all yours."

"I'll be in my office when you're ready."

Smith walked back out to the foyer, engaging in a conversation with Marilyn. The bit of privacy gave Gareth time to settle into the guest office. He took a couple of contracts out of his briefcase that one of his lawyers asked him to sign and scan back by the end of the day. There were a couple of phone calls he needed to place as well, but he'd wait until Cynthia made an appearance.

The protein smoothie he'd bought would only last so long. He glanced at his watch, noting the time. Cynthia should have arrived by now. He didn't bother to close the blinds, seeing that the large floor to ceiling window gave him a wide-open view of the foyer. It would be nice to see her smiling face coming toward him first thing.

Smith's reappearance caught Gareth by surprise. The man's expression said everything, bringing Gareth to his feet.

"You might want to give Cynthia a call," Smith said in a rather grim tone. "My father just gave me a heads up. Detective Nielsen is about to bring Kurt Langston into the police station for questioning in regard to Brad's murder."

CYNTHIA GAVE HER apartment a quick glance, satisfied with the way it looked. The modern décor fit her personality, along with the antiques she'd been able to sprinkle in throughout the blended arrangement. The design was rather unique and fit her personality. She was rather meticulous, but there had been a few odds and ends she'd needed to do before bringing Gareth home this evening.

It was time to have a conversation that his hotel room was no longer needed.

Gareth's home base was in New York, where his family still resided. Lately, he'd been spending more and more time in Minneapolis. He always stayed at The Foshay, but she planned on surprising him today with his own key to her apartment. After this weekend, and basically the last month, there was no reason to wait a second longer.

Cynthia grabbed her keys off the artistic bowl she'd purchased at one of the art museums downtown. She tucked the grey clutch purse she'd decided to use due to the slate coloring matching the pantsuit she'd changed into after her shower. The black heels she'd chosen to wear on Friday had been such good luck that she preferred to keep the momentum moving steadily forward.

Another quick glance in the mirror she'd hung in her small entryway, and she was ready to face the day.

Or so she thought.

It didn't take her long to ride the elevator downstairs, having taken only a moment to speak with Mrs. Ganglia. The elderly woman had collected her mail and was making her way to her apartment. It was rare that Cynthia was ever running this late, so she took advantage of the moment and stopped to chat about the upcoming winter the meteorologists were warning would be a bitter one.

"You take care of yourself, Mrs. Ganglia. I'm sure I'll see you at one of the holiday luncheons."

Cynthia had used the parking garage when she'd pulled in this morning, so she veered in that direction versus walking toward the main lobby. A smile blossomed on her lips as she thought about Gareth's reaction to the extra key she'd tucked into the inside zippered pocket of her purse.

He'd told her that he loved her.

No other man had ever said those three words to her.

In that moment, her thoughts had been so scrambled that she'd kissed him—fervently. One thing led to another until neither one of them spoke for hours, and the time never felt right to reciprocate those words. She certainly didn't want to say them during sex, and then they'd gotten to sharing their pasts and talking about their dreams for the future.

The lone key she was about to give him should speak volumes, but she'd rehearsed a small speech that would leave no doubt where she stood in this relationship.

"Cynthia, do you have a moment?"

She had to be hearing things. Cynthia stopped just short of the glass door that led to the parking garage. There was just enough reflection in the glass to make out the man who'd called her name from behind her.

Karma really was a bitch.

"Kurt, what the hell are you doing here at my apartment

building?"

Cynthia took her time in facing the one person she could have gone the rest of her life without ever setting eyes on again. Nausea caused a couple of waves in her stomach, and she was grateful that she hadn't had time to drink her usual glass of orange juice this morning. The added acid would have done the trick.

Kurt had aged in the three years since she'd last seen him, though it was to his advantage. The greying edges made him appear even more prominent and trustworthy than before, camouflaging that he was nothing but a wolf in sheep's clothing.

Why was it that men who began to grey early were considered distinguished and women just looked older?

It was blatantly unfair.

"We need to talk about that letter you turned in to the police."

Cynthia debated on whether or not to allow him to believe that she was the one who had contacted Detective Nielsen, but then thought better of it.

There'd been enough lies between the two of them.

She wouldn't resort to his level.

"I had nothing to do with the discovery of that particular letter." Cynthia tightened her grip on the keys in her hand. She was still coming to terms with his audacity to seek her out at her home. He had no right, but this wasn't a fight she was willing to have first thing this morning. "Whatever you have to say can be said to the police. We have nothing to discuss. Please excuse me."

"Cynthia, I admit that I didn't want my wife to found out about our affair, but—"

"You make it sound like I was even slightly aware that we were having an extramarital affair," Cynthia corrected, unable to

go with her original decision to drop this subject matter. She
hated to lose, and this was turning into a battle of wills. "I was
clearly deceived into believing we had a relationship. By you. So,
I would suggest being very careful on how you word your
statement to the police, because it's already been proven that you
have a track record of bending the facts to get what you want."

"That letter to Brad Manon was not about you." Kurt
glanced behind him, though it wasn't like anyone else was in the
foyer. It was then Cynthia noticed the manner in which he was
massaging the back of his neck. He was nervous. "It was about
Phil Colbert."

Cynthia had been in this business long enough to learn to
never let her opponent see that he or she had the best of her.
Phil Colbert? What the hell was Kurt talking about? A brief
moment to digest the news was all she allowed herself before
responding.

"Again, whatever you have to say can be said to the authorities."

Cynthia turned to go, never expecting Kurt to reach for her.
The grip on her arm was tight enough to immediately bring her
level of awareness to one of defense.

"You have one second to remove your hand or else I'll make
sure that you'll be in pain for the rest of the day," Cynthia
threatened, ready to drop her purse and keys to do what was
necessary. Some would label her a health nut with her whole-
some diet and daily exercise. She'd taken several self-defense
classes and was perfectly capable of defending herself against a
dandy like Kurt. "One…"

Kurt immediately dropped his hand and stepped back, appearing more offended than had she told him to go fuck himself.
She still reserved the right to do so.

"I'm trying to save both of our firms, Cynthia. If I go down,

Manon Investments goes down with me. It's the reason I wrote the letter in the first place. You—"

"Kurt Langston?"

Cynthia had been so focused on what Kurt was suggesting that she hadn't noticed Detective Nielsen and two uniformed officers walking through the lobby.

"Kurt, what is it that you need to say about Phil Colbert?" Cynthia had lowered her voice, gauging the distance between them and the police. She decided it was better to get answers before the firm was blindsided by another scandal. "Tell me now."

"You really don't know?"

There was a bit of relief that crossed Kurt's chiseled features, but Cynthia sensed he still doubted her response. Unfortunately, she ran out of time to obtain any more information.

"Mr. Langston, you're a hard man to track down." Detective Nielsen observed what had to appear as some type of cover-up meeting. If Cynthia wasn't careful, she was going to follow in Grace's footsteps that led directly to a prison a cell. "Your assistant was gracious enough to call your driver, who in turn led us directly to Ms. Ellsworth's door."

Cynthia remained quiet, not wanting to comment on a topic she didn't have all the facts on without an attorney present. She'd seen the trouble Laurel and Grace had to deal with in regard to Brad's murder. Vital knowledge had been learned during that time—such as always have a lawyer present.

"Cynthia and I are old friends," Kurt explained with a rigid smile, tightening the belt around his dress coat. "How may I help you, Detective?"

"I have some questions for you. I also believe that the interview should be conducted at the station."

Detective Nielsen let his gaze linger on Cynthia, most likely waiting for her to verify Kurt's claim on why he was in her apartment building. She held steady on her black high heels.

"I'm sure you'll understand that I need to contact my lawyer before answering any of your questions." Kurt wasn't a man who minced words. Neither was he one who wasted time, which was why it didn't surprise her when he brushed past the detective as if this entire matter was an inconvenience. Any fear he displayed earlier was gone. "I'm a busy man, Detective, as you well know. Let's get this over with so that I can get to my own business."

Cynthia was lucky that Detective Nielsen hadn't taken her into the station for questioning as well, but that didn't mean she got away without a warning.

"Ms. Ellsworth, I'm sure you're well aware of the reason I'm bringing Mr. Langston in for questioning. Is there anything you'd like to tell me before this goes any further?"

"Meredith Manon came into my office Friday morning with a copy of a letter she'd found in Brad's home office." Cynthia had nothing to hide. Had Kurt not shown up at her apartment building this morning, she wouldn't even have known that the letter had nothing to do with her. "I told her the same thing I'm going to tell you. Kurt and I had an affair three years ago. I did *not* know that he was married, and I ended things the moment I found out. As to what the letter was in regard to, you'll have to ask him. I have nothing more to say on this matter."

Detective Nielsen nodded after she'd finished speaking, though she was sure this wasn't the last she'd see of him in the coming days. His speculative expression told that he didn't quite believe her explanation. They said their goodbyes, and Cynthia watched on as he and the two officers took their leave.

Numerous thoughts ran through her mind as she tried to prioritize her day.

First thing on the agenda?

Cynthia was going to call one of the top criminal defense lawyers in town.

CHAPTER NINE

"HOW WERE YOU, of all people, able to obtain Justin Monroe as your attorney?" Smith asked, sitting down in one of the high back leather swivel chairs surrounding the conference room table. "He told me that there was a conflict of interest to take on any more clients regarding this case."

"And one of the reasons Justin mentioned the conflict of interest to you was because I hired him the second Grace had all charges dropped against her. It's amazing what a few crisp dollars can get you these days."

Gareth admired the way Cynthia handled the multitude of questions thrown her way after she'd shown up at the office. She'd quickly herded all those close to the situation into the conference room, though he didn't miss the frown of displeasure Marilyn tried to hide. He had to wonder when her staged revolt would eventually take place.

He was still reeling from the fact that Kurt Langston had the balls to show up at Cynthia's apartment after what he'd done to her. The guy was a real class act, and one Gareth wanted to ensure was brought to his knees.

Unfortunately, it appeared that the police and media had dibs, but Gareth knew that revenge was a dish best served cold.

The last segment of the news Gareth had seen before Cynthia had strolled through the glass doors of Manon Investments with her head held high was the fact that the press had surrounded Kurt Langston's residence. His wife would now know for certain that she'd married a lying, cheating asshole—as if she didn't already know that deep down inside.

Cynthia had been right all along about someone leaking this to the press.

"Are you saying you anticipated that you'd need Justin's services?" Paul asked as he ventured into an allied minefield. What the hell was wrong with him? "Cynthia, now is the time to let me know if any more surprises are coming down the pike. If you know something the rest of us don't, you should tell us now."

Gareth walked past Cynthia's chair, brushing his fingers over her shoulder in an attempt to ward off what could potentially be a rather heated discussion. Paul had all but accused her of knowing something probative about Brad's murder. That wasn't going to go over well with the present company.

"Paul, it's called covering one's ass. You should be familiar with that particular preventative measure. You've used it on numerous occasions yourself." Cynthia leaned back in the black chair and crossed her legs. He could easily see that she was controlling the narrative. She'd rested her hands on the arms of the chair as she took in each and every individual in attendance. Gareth walked over to the window overlooking the city and leaned against the sill to watch the rest of the conversation play out. He could easily picture Cynthia wearing a crown to denote her place at the head of the table. "What I'd like to know is if any of you are aware of a connection between Kurt Langston and Phil Colbert."

A round of negative replies went around the group that included Paul, Smith, Laurel, and Grace. This small assembly was obviously made up of those individuals Cynthia trusted, but Gareth doubted that she'd get the answers she sought.

"Cynthia, why don't we call Phil in here and ask him directly? He's a good guy."

"Because that would be interfering with an active homicide investigation, much like Meredith attempted to do by coming to me with that letter on Friday." Cynthia compressed her lips together to smooth out her lipstick in a habit he'd taken notice of months ago. She only did so when she was deep in thought. "Paul, Phil has always been Manon Investments' go-to technology analyst. Grace has spent the last hour searching our records for any trades involving Kurt's tech company. I came up empty. Do you remember if it was ever discussed out in the trading room or behind closed doors with Brad?"

"No, but I was rarely in those meetings Brad had with the analysts regarding stock picks." Paul sat back in his chair and held his hands up in the current setback. "We could—"

Cynthia cocked an eyebrow, all but daring him to suggest they bring Phil into the loop.

"What about Steve?" Smith suggested, looking around the room for anyone on board with the new idea. "He's been here from the initial opening of the fund, and he attended most of those meetings."

"We're starting to sound a bit paranoid," Laurel interjected, sharing a look with Grace. "We have no proof that Kurt's letter has anything to do with Brad's murder. I know he came to your apartment building this morning, Cynthia, but we can't assume anything unless the police find proof that whatever business Kurt conducted with Brad led to his death."

Everyone began talking at once. Gareth wasn't involved in the business side of things, other than his money was at stake along with every other investor based on the decisions this firm made since inception. From a business angle, whatever Kurt Langston had done or hadn't done wouldn't be so obvious.

"We might be looking in the wrong direction." Gareth waited until all eyes fell on him. "We're assuming that letter had something to do with Kurt's company, but what if it's about another tech firm? Who was his competition back then?"

The silence was deafening.

Gareth now had all eyes on him, but it was Cynthia's smile that told him he might have just found something to make all their troubles go away.

"Grace?"

Cynthia only had to say her friend's name to garner the appropriate response.

"On it," Grace quickly replied, already out of her seat and walking toward the door.

"I'll give Detective Nielsen a call to let him know what could potentially be at stake," Smith shared before he followed quickly behind Grace, though not before brushing his hand across Laurel's shoulder. Had Gareth not been looking, he wouldn't have seen the intimate exchange. "Maybe he'll let something slip about his conversation with Langston."

"Cynthia, is there anything I can do?" Laurel asked, her concern evident for Cynthia on a much personal level. "You realize it's only a matter of time before the media descends on us again, right?"

"I know, which is why I'm going to come up with a statement before Kurt Langston has the ability to spin this media circus in his direction."

Gareth continued to sit back and listen as Cynthia discussed various methods with Laurel and Paul that would allow Manon Investments to control the narrative. She was a born leader and right in her element at the helm.

Sure, she wasn't on the board of Manon Investments, but it was clear her opinion held a massive amount of weight. It was also evident that she enjoyed her career, though Gareth couldn't help but stop to think about the change she could implement in the various charities his family held sway over.

With Cynthia's attitude and perseverance, the two of them could change the world.

"I'll contact the journalist who hosts the financial news during the morning premarket blitz." Cynthia had decided what tactic to take after several were debated between the other two employees at the table. Gareth noted that the board members had not been a part of this meeting, which had him wondering if Paul had attended to clue them in on what had transpired during this morning's strategy session. "Paul, don't inform the board of this. Not yet. Give me time to get the phone interview rolled out so that no one can throw a wrench into the works on this and leave us hanging out to dry."

That set off another five minutes of discussions and what the plan would be if any of this backfired on them, but Cynthia had a pretty damn good handle on the situation. It wasn't long before the conference room cleared out, leaving Gareth alone with Cynthia.

"Do you really believe that Brad and Phil made some type of bid to sabotage another tech company?" Cynthia remained seated, her blue gaze remaining steady on him as he finally moved away from the windowsill. "They could have taken a short position in another tech firm, running the price of the stock down. For what purpose, though? A takeover? I don't recall Kurt ever talking about a takeover or merger with another firm."

Gareth figured Kurt Langston wasn't a man to mix business with pleasure.

"I know this isn't what you want to hear right now," Gareth said, pulling up the chair that Paul had vacated. He rolled a bit closer so that he could lean forward and take ahold of her hands. What he was about to suggest was rather crass, but he'd never met a more self-assured woman. "Is there a chance here that Langston got involved with you just to give him additional leverage over Brad?"

"It's all I've thought of since our run in this morning."

Gareth was already in tune with where her thoughts were taking her. He didn't like it, but he understood her need to speak with Langston again…only this time without a police presence bearing down on them.

"You're not going to be alone with that man," Gareth warned, unsure of how much danger she could be putting herself in by walking down this path. A man was already dead, others had been dragged through the mud, and a firm was about to be under siege. "I want to be with you when you confront him."

"I—"

Neither one of them were expecting the conference door to open, which caused them both to immediately look that direction.

"Cynthia, could I speak with you in private?" Phil Colbert stood in the doorway pushing his black-rimmed glasses up the bridge of his nose. "In my office?"

"Of course," Cynthia replied, releasing Gareth's hands and rolling the chair backward with the back of her knees. "I'll be there in a minute."

Both Gareth and Cynthia waited for Phil to close the conference room door, but it was evident he wasn't pleased with the delay.

"So help me…make that Paul Salter…if he went to Phil without allowing me to look into this matter first," Cynthia muttered, turning back to face Gareth with annoyance. This wasn't how they'd pictured the first workday after such a wonderful weekend. Then again, it had been foolish to assume that anything could move forward until the individual who murdered Brad Manon was behind bars. "I'll make his life a living hell."

"You don't know why Phil wants to speak with you. It might not be about anything related to Langston." Gareth was somewhat removed from this business matter, but that didn't mean he hadn't made a few phone calls regarding Langston and his business. It was always better to know everything one could about one's adversary before going to battle. "I said it before, and I'll say it again. I want you to watch your back, Cyn. Someone had the ability to get into the building's security feed and shut it down for a night. Speaking with Smith, I'm inclined to agree it's someone that is employed by Manon Investments."

CHAPTER TEN

C YNTHIA STOPPED BY her own office first to make the phone calls required to set up the phone interview, not surprised in the least that the network jumped at the chance. This wasn't the route she'd wanted to take, but it was better than the alternative of turning the initiative over to Langston. There was no way in hell she was going to allow Kurt Langston's past misdeeds to interfere with her personal or professional future.

"Cynthia, do you have a moment?" Vern asked after he materialized in her doorway.

She stifled her immediate response, which would have been *hell no.* But Vern wasn't responsible for the lack of time she had in the day. Her stomach growled, reminding her that she never drank that smoothie Gareth had sitting on the desk in the guest office. Lunch was still at least an hour away, though she doubted she'd have time to eat anything.

"I have a meeting with Phil, but I can spare a minute or two," Cynthia said honestly, hoping to curtail whatever topic Vern needed to cover today. "What's up?"

Cynthia wished she'd stayed behind her desk so that she could take a seat, because Vern quietly closed her office door. That could only mean that this conversation was going to take a hell of a lot longer than sixty seconds. She used her desk as leverage, leaning against the edge as she rested her palms on either side of her.

"I wanted to be upfront with you before this situation gets out of hand."

Vern leaned against the door, his graying combover causing him to look older than he really was at the age of fifty-one. His years of experience was the reason Rye Marshall put an offer on the table, though Grace had mentioned that Vern had been the one to seek out the other firm. No one could blame him, considering that Brad hadn't been easy to work with in the last few years of his life.

If Vern wanted to get something off his chest, then it appeared that Marilyn may have been talking out of turn. The receptionist was the glue that held this company together, but that didn't mean she didn't miscalculate when prying into the private lives of the employees. The woman always had her ear to the ground and her eye on the prize.

"You know about my upcoming interview regarding Kurt Langston," Cynthia said, deciding to cut right to the chase. "For the record, I asked Paul to keep it under wraps with regard to the board until the segment airs. This is on me, and the board is going to have to accept my decision for doing the interview. It's better to get out in front of this before Kurt can swing the narrative his direction. I won't have my professional life sullied by that cheating bastard and his bag full of lies."

Cynthia waited for Vern to become judgmental, all but accusing Cynthia of being the woman Kurt cheated with on his wife. It wouldn't be a lie, but no one ever bothered to hear both sides of the story before jumping on the bandwagon.

Grace and Laurel were constantly telling her that she needed to have more faith in people, but that was hard when everyone seemed so hellbent on proving her right in her original assessment.

"Cynthia, you're a straight shooter. I appreciate that more

than you know, which is why you don't need to hide the fact that you're aware of my offer to go to work for Marshall Securities. I'm taking it." Vern hesitated, almost as if he were about to change his mind as to why he'd come to talk to you. "I've spoken to Detective Nielsen at length regarding this transition and the reasons why."

Cynthia braced herself for more bad news, and that was saying something.

"It's common knowledge that Brad changed after his divorce from Meredith, and not for the better. They both claimed to remain good friends, but we all know how that kind of crap goes. His mood swings set people on edge, he began taking chances that were a bit too risky for even some of the analysts' positions, and he started gambling with his personal savings on the side."

Vern wasn't telling Cynthia anything she didn't already know, and that included the bit about the gambling. Everyone was well aware of Brad's personal vices, and those weren't few. Hell, the first thing she thought of when she'd gotten the call from Grace regarding Brad's death was that he'd gotten into debt with the wrong people.

One thing stood out that she wanted to clarify before Vern left the firm.

"You realize that those professional risks Brad wanted to take panned out, don't you?" Cynthia wasn't so tense now that she'd been made aware of the territory they were entering. "Upon the analysts' disagreements with some of the trades Brad wanted to make back then, he decided to execute them himself through his own personal account. Seeing as the firm held no shares in those companies, he was completely free and clear to execute them personally. Bottom line? He made a pretty hefty profit for himself. It was when he began withdrawing funds from his 401k to increase his odds that he ran down his account. In the end, he took too many risks and drained his personal funds."

It was at that exact moment that she realized what they'd all overlooked.

How could she have missed it before?

"Vern, I could kiss you." Cynthia quickly walked over to her credenza and opened the drawer. It didn't take her long to find the folder, but what was inside brought her up short. "Fuck."

"Brad's past choices are what I wanted to speak with you about," Vern said, stepping forward and waving one hand in the air rather helplessly as he ignored her slight panic. "I figured that impromptu meeting of yours had something to do with Phil, but I thought you should know the entire story."

Vern's words barely registered as Cynthia continued to stare at the folder that was relatively empty. Someone had snuck into her office, somehow broken into her filing cabinet, and taken the personal trade sheets she'd personally signed off on during a specific time period—three years ago, to be precise.

The entire story…

"Vern, what are you talking about?"

Cynthia didn't have to look at the modern style clock she'd hung up on her office wall to know that she had less than hour to get ready for the interview. The anchor wanted to air it during the lunch hour so that they could dominate that market share during a prime time slot. At this rate, the only news that was about to be shared over the airwaves was the fact that Manon Investments was once again the target of a criminal conspiracy.

What she needed to do was place an immediate call into Detective Nielsen, but she had a gut feeling that Vern was about to make an already complicated situation even more convoluted.

"I personally overheard Phil talking to Brad a few weeks

before his death about investing in Kurt Langston's tech company," Vern said with a disapproving frown. "I didn't think anything of it at the time, because I figured Phil would run it by you to ensure he met the firm's compliance policy in doing so. But then this morning I heard from Marilyn about you and…well, it was then I realized there could be a connection to Brad's death."

"Vern, you're still a board member," Cynthia reminded him rather cautiously, needing to buy time until Detective Nielsen could look into this situation. "I want you to gather everyone in the conference room for a meeting. I don't care what excuse you give, but I want Phil Colbert in that room."

Vern muttered something under his breath when he realized that Cynthia wasn't kidding around about congregating the staff. She could have sworn he mentioned something about this being one of the reasons he needed to leave this place, and she might have actually heard the words *insane fucking people* in there somewhere.

"Steve can't—"

"I know Steve can't leave his position on the desk, but everyone else can get their asses in the conference room immediately," Cynthia demanded, having a hell of a morning already. Vern still had responsibilities to this firm. "I'll call Detective Nielsen. This is something he should know, as well as the fact that someone broke into my files and has stolen some of the firm's financial records."

Now that garnered Vern's attention. His grayish blue eyes dropped to the folder in her hand, and the creases in his forehead deepened even more.

Both of them turned to her office door when a knock sounded, and Cynthia held her breath after she'd called out for whoever it was to enter. She wasn't ready to deal with Phil and the fact that he could very well be involved with whatever had taken place between Brad and Kurt three years ago.

She exhaled slowly with relief when it was Blair who opened the door.

"Cynthia, I wanted your opinion on—" Blair stopped short, catching sight of Vern. "Oh, I'm sorry. I thought you said to come in. I didn't mean to interrupt your meeting."

"It's fine," Cynthia assured her, closing the file in her hand. It did dawn on her that there could be fingerprints that Detective Nielsen could lift in order to determine who accessed the files. She carefully set it down on top of the credenza. "Actually, Vern is calling a meeting in the conference room with the entire staff. Can we talk later?"

"Of course," Blair responded with a curious glance toward Vern. She gave a small shrug, holding up her coffee mug. "I'll just go and grab a fresh cup and pass the word."

"I'll round up the rest of the crew," Vern said begrudgingly after Blair vacated the doorway. "I hope you know what you're doing."

No, she didn't. She didn't have all the angles covered.

Cynthia had absolutely no idea what she was doing, other than calling the detective to sort out this matter in case Phil was the guilty party. Did she believe that Phil was capable of committing murder? No, but she'd been wrong about many things in the recent past.

"Cyn?"

Gareth's voice was a welcome relief. She would have given almost anything to go back to when they were at the hotel in bed with their legs entwined and having not a care in the world. Kurt Langston had been a blip on her radar, long gone off the screen. She'd finally opened up to Gareth about that painful time in her life, and she'd thought their future was assured.

"Just when I think it can't get any worse," Cynthia muttered, walking into Gareth's embrace. She closed her eyes and savored the intoxicating scent of his cologne. "You were right."

"About?"

"I might have actually worked side by side for years with the very man who killed Brad." Cynthia gave herself thirty more seconds before pulling away from the security of his arms. It was time she called Detective Nielsen. "I think Kurt's business wasn't going well, and he somehow talked Phil into investing into his tech company. It makes me believe that whatever happened three years ago to prompt Kurt to write that letter had nothing to do with me, and everything to do with Phil Colbert and his actions."

CHAPTER ELEVEN

G ARETH LEANED BACK in his desk chair as he studied the uniformed officer who'd accompanied Detective Nielsen. It wasn't long after his arrival that the so-called staff meeting in the conference room had been broken up with Phil, Vern, and Cynthia remaining behind with the detective.

Paul had expressed his concern, as well as Steve, but Detective Nielsen had controlled the situation expertly to elicit as much information as he could before anyone thought to lawyer up. Board members held no sway over police investigations, so they weren't able to interfere. Honestly, not even Paul was foolish enough to push the detective too far.

"Marilyn ordered lunch to be delivered in an hour," Laurel said, appearing in the doorway looking anything but hungry. He didn't miss that she'd swept her hair over her shoulder, which she tended to do when stressed. Cynthia had mentioned it a time or two, saying her friend should cut it shorter so that it didn't bother her when wearing it down. "Grace called Justin Monroe. He was her attorney when she was falsely arrested. I'm thinking I should give Meg Preston a call. She is Smith's attorney, and I'm not so sure anyone should be talking to Detective Mancini without representation."

Another detective had arrived not five minutes ago, but he'd asked to speak with Smith in private. Gareth had found it odd, but he assumed it was all part of Detective Nielsen's plan to split the employees to garner as much information as he could. Wasn't it better to divide and conquer?

"I'm sure Smith has already told the other detective that he won't be answering any questions without a lawyer present," Gareth assured her, not surprised when she took a seat in the guest chair. "Smith's father probably grilled that into his head from a very young age."

"I know, and we've already been through this multiple times since…"

It was easy to forget that Laurel had been the one to find Brad dead with his throat slit at his desk. That sight wasn't just something someone got over in the span of a month or two. It would no doubt haunt her dreams for the rest of her life.

Gareth might not have been close to his brother, but no one deserved to die choking on their own blood as the lights went out. The funeral had been a sad affair, though Meredith had put together a beautiful ceremony. Gareth had never really gotten to know her well, but that had been more Brad's doing.

"I don't even know why Detective Mancini would want to speak with Smith, considering the animosity between the two of them."

"I'm sorry?" Gareth wasn't sure what Laurel was referring to, other than maybe the detective didn't appreciate having to deal with a judge's son in a murder investigation. "Did this Detective Mancini have a run-in with Judge Gallo?"

"More like a run-in with Smith's younger brother," Laurel said rather wryly, though she did so with a fond smile. "Sebastian got into a fight down at a club called First Ave. The charges were dropped."

Gareth didn't have to ask if the charges were dropped because of Sebastian's last name. No officer wanted to get on Judge Gallo's bad side, even though he would never expect his children to be treated differently than anyone else's progeny. The law was the law. But the man couldn't control the actions of others, and some of Smith's siblings benefited from that small privilege.

"Is this where the party is?" Grace asked good-naturedly, but her attempt fell flat. She walked into the office and took a seat next to Laurel. "I'm wondering if we shouldn't call Justin. Smith's been holed up in his office with that detective for around ten minutes now. What do you think they're talking about?"

"I don't know, but each minute that passes causes my headache to get worse," Laurel muttered, tapping her manicured nails on the wooden arms of the chair. "Okay. My patience is worn thin. I'm going to go and call Meg Preston. She was with Smith during the initial questioning. This waiting is giving me an ulcer."

Grace must have received a text. She held up her phone and quickly replied, though Gareth didn't miss that her gaze kept drifting toward the door. It hadn't escaped his notice that Blair had walked past twice in the past five minutes. He didn't know much about her, but that was about to change after the call he'd placed this morning.

"Do you know Kurt Langston?"

Grace arched one of her blonde brows as she finally finished sending her text. It was evident that she thought he'd asked because of Cynthia. There might be a bit of truth to that, but he was more concerned with the fact that the man could be a sociopath.

"I've never met him, but Cynthia would never have—"

"I know that Cynthia would never have gotten involved with Langston had she known he was married or what kind of character he really had," Gareth clarified, rubbing his lower lip with this thumb. Something didn't sit right with him about this entire situation. "Cynthia told me over the weekend that she'd been having dinner with Brad and Paul regarding Phil Colbert when she'd met Langston three years ago. Now, every single one of these people are being tied together after Brad's death. Coincidence is one thing, but don't you think this is a stretch?"

"You have a good point, but think about the other scenarios." Grace cradled the cell phone in her hand as she made herself comfortable in the chair. It was a good thing her job was slow this time of day. "Steve was having an affair with Meredith. We also can't forget that Josh came back to the office that night to tell Brad about the affair. He was basically the last person to see Brad alive. Then there's the fact that Brad was in debt to some very unsavory people from what I've heard."

"What about the others?" Gareth asked, taking a quick glance at his watch. He was expecting to hear back from his source today regarding a quick background check on everyone employed at Manon Investments. He was stepping outside his bounds, but Cynthia had been drawn into a game of office roulette…at least, that's how she referenced it a time or two. He couldn't just stand back and wait for the loaded chamber to spin back around. "Blair? Vern? Marilyn?"

"Actually, my stepbrother was front and center last week," Grace confessed, shifting in unease. "Brandon is out on parole for insider trading, but someone…somehow…pointed the police in his direction. Someone is manipulating this investigation."

"The same person who framed you for murder." Gareth rested his arm on the desk, picking up a pen for something to tap. He always thought better when doing something mindlessly. "Meredith was the one who turned a letter dated over three years ago to the police. She was the one who turned the course of this investigation. Unknowingly or with purpose, who knows?"

"Trust me, every face flashed through my mind when I was sitting in that jail cell," Grace muttered, tucking a flyaway hair behind her ear. "The scary thing is that It's clear that whoever killed Brad is working hard at throwing everyone else under the bus. And there are things Langston couldn't have known unless…"

"Unless what?" Gareth asked, resting the end of the pen on the folder in front of him. "Cynthia told me about your false alibi for Rye Marshall, and how no one could have known that unless they'd overheard you talking with Cynthia and Laurel."

"Exactly. So, how would Kurt Langston know enough to set me up without someone on the inside?"

"Phil Colbert."

"Or Meredith. She was here the morning that I confessed to Cynthia and Laurel about what I'd done for Rye. But again, you and I are attempting to do the same thing the rest of the staff have been doing—guessing. It's all a guessing game."

The last thing Gareth expected was for Grace to be smiling after their conversation. She even let out a light laugh, which was rather unsettling.

"What's so funny?" Laurel asked, rejoining them. She didn't reclaim her seat, but instead leaned against the doorframe. It gave her the ability to keep an eye on Smith's office door. "Oh, and I left a message for Meg Preston. She wasn't in her office."

"Gareth tossed Marilyn's name in the ring." Grace laughed again, but this time Gareth was able to sense the underlying exhaustion. "I couldn't imagine that sweet woman killing anyone, let alone Brad. She's been here since the inception of the firm."

"Marilyn keeps her cards close to her chest," Laurel admitted with a slight shrug, lowering her voice so that it didn't carry out into the foyer. "Don't let her fool you. I can understand why you would think she could have the opportunity to commit murder, but she has nothing to gain from it."

"You're thinking about it from a greed angle, but it could simply be that someone just snapped. I've seen it happen time and again over the smallest of things. An unintentional slight of some sort," Gareth shared, having been in places where the wrong look could get a person killed. "Anyone can snap."

Gareth's cell phone finally rang.

"Nicollet."

"I sent the files to your email." The long pause on the other end of the line prevented Gareth from disconnecting the call. "And you might want to turn on the news. Kurt Langston was in a car accident after leaving the police station. He's in ICU in critical condition. His driver didn't make it."

CHAPTER TWELVE

"I'LL GET IT," Grace said after hearing the doorbell ring, standing up from one of the twin La-Z-Boy overstuffed chairs near the fireplace. "It's probably the pizza delivery boy."

Cynthia shared a look with Gareth, all but telling him that she wasn't going to be able to eat a thing this evening. Even the thought of food made her stomach roll as if she were riding a tiny dinghy in a storm ravaged sea. Actually, she'd rather be vacationing on a yacht in the middle of the Mediterranean Ocean, sunbathing in a tiny bikini off the coast of Sicily if it only meant not dealing with the reality that was now her life.

"I had Grace order some breadsticks, too. You shouldn't drink wine on an empty stomach, but I figured that red sauce might not be such a good idea." Gareth gave her an endearing half smile. "Besides, there's garlic and onion powder on those breadsticks. I can't be the only one with abhorrent breath."

Gareth had removed his suit jacket and was in the process of rolling up his sleeves. They'd all decided to drive to Rye Marshall's residence after work today, especially given the circumstances of Kurt Langston's medical condition. As far as everyone knew, the man was still in critical condition.

"So, catch me up on what Phil Colbert said about Kurt Langston." Rye had entered the living room carrying paper plates and napkins. He set them on the coffee table, but made sure there was room for the boxes of pizza and sides. "Grace kept me apprised via texts, but I'm sure there was more to it than Phil and Kurt being longtime friends."

Cynthia was the only one in the room who could answer Rye, considering no one else had been with her in the meeting other than Vern and Phil. Her temples began to throb at recalling the first five minutes of the conversation, let alone the end when Vern all but demanded Phil's resignation.

That was the moment Paul had been needed in the meeting, and then things just got worse from there.

"Phil Colbert had invested money into Kurt's startup tech firm over eight years ago, but he didn't tell anyone at the firm. He made quite a profit on it when the company went public," Cynthia shared, settling back into Gareth when he'd joined her on the couch. "Apparently, Phil cashed out before anyone was the wiser that he'd broken compliance rules by not reporting such an investment to me."

"Vern explained to the board members today that Kurt Langston wrote that letter to Brad as a way of covering his ass if any of that got out, because three years ago was when Phil quietly reinvested quite a bit of money to drive up the share price. Colbert and Langston basically manipulated the stock, presumably with Brad in on it with one of his personal accounts. At least, that's what Vern is assuming. The SEC shouldn't have a problem proving all of this once they get access to their personal accounts. Bottom line was that Langston wasn't going to go down all alone," Smith added on, taking a paper plate from the stack. Grace had returned with the pizzas, stepping back when she realized it was basically a free for all. "It's quite sad that Vern's last day at Manon Investments was firing an analyst who has been with the firm since the beginning."

"I'll make sure Vern has a good first day tomorrow," Rye said with a satisfied smile. He stepped back and took a seat in the chair before Grace could backhand him. "Okay, okay. I'll be good from now on."

"Like that's ever going to happen," Grace muttered good-naturedly, picking up her wineglass from the side table and taking a seat on the opposite side of the couch. "Smith's going to fire me for sure if you decide to steal any more of our employees."

"I wouldn't fire you, because then you'd go work for him," Smith shot back, sitting back on the loveseat with two slices of pizza. "That would ultimately be counterproductive. I can't have that happen on my watch. That reminds me, we need to sit down and talk about your current bonus structure."

Laughter floated around the group as these two competitive men were now in direct competition over a pizza pie shared among friends. In around eight to nine months, Smith would be taking on the majority of Manon Investments' clients under a new hedge fund operated by Gallo Capital Management. He took Vern's leaving personally, but the man needed a clean slate after everything that had happened in the past couple of months.

"Cynthia, I know it doesn't seem like it now," Laurel said, turning the discussion back to the topic at hand, "but this is good news. That letter had nothing to do about the relationship between you and Kurt Langston. Smith was able to step into the interview without anyone the wiser. He explained the changes that were coming down the pike in regard to the new fund, as well as touching on the subject of bringing in fresh blood. In the end, it all worked out for the best."

"It's going to be a shitstorm when the SEC comes through the doors after what Phil and Kurt cooked up," Smith said with disgust, though it didn't appear as if he'd lost his appetite over the coming storm. "But it's better to do this now while the firm is still Manon Investments. It's an easier sell to the media, and we've already come clean with all the clients. Those who will transition over have expressed their belief in the new leadership plan and are optimistic toward future gains."

One of the reasons they all hadn't been able to compare notes on the day was the fact that she and Smith had spent the majority of the afternoon calling each and every client regarding Phil Colbert's illegal actions and his recent dismissal.

She hadn't had any time to process the fact that Kurt was in a car accident and currently lying in a hospital bed in the ICU desperately hanging on for his life.

It wasn't that the tragedy involved her in any way, but something didn't sit right with her about the accident. She didn't want to admit it, but the thought had crossed her mind that Phil might have had something to do with the accident and very possibly Brad's death, as well. Otherwise, it was one hell of a coincidence, wasn't it?

And that thought led her to another issue she hadn't tackled yet.

"I can't believe you had the balls to have a background check done on every person I work with," Cynthia said, lowering her voice as the others carried on the conversation about the upcoming SEC investigation into Phil's wrongdoing. "I could have told you what you needed to know if you needed that reassurance."

Well, not *everything* there was to know. No one had known that Phil was using an offshore account under his wife's maiden name to dabble in the market outside of her oversight as compliance manager, and all because he didn't want to have to comply with SEC regulations that the firm was required to follow. The nail into Phil Colbert's coffin had been admitting to manipulating the stock, though he swore on his life that he had nothing to do with Brad's murder.

Cynthia leaned forward so that Gareth could fill a couple of plates for them. He handed off a few breadsticks to her before taking two slices of pizza for himself.

"You don't seem to have a problem with the fact that there are two agents sitting outside in a vehicle in order to keep an eye on Grace," Gareth said wryly, removing the glass of wine from her hand so that he could set it down on the coffee table. "A man was murdered in your workplace and a friend of yours was subsequently framed for homicide. The list goes on, but I can't just sit back and do nothing. Besides, nothing stood out in those files I was sent today. Honestly, Rye's decision to hire additional security isn't such a bad idea. We just don't know what is coming around the next corner."

"I know you don't want to talk about Kurt Langston, but has there been any news on what happened with the car accident?" Rye asked, having already finished off one of his slices. He crossed his ankle over his knee, settling back in the chair to digest both the pizza and the conversation. "I can't be the only one who finds it awfully coincidental that another individual involved in this case almost lost his life today, not to mention that his driver was killed."

"The same thought crossed my mind," Cynthia said, not meaning to come off distracted. She was busy trying to figure out what time Phil came into the office today, but she hadn't been in early herself to know that information. Could he have tampered with Kurt's vehicle? The thought itself seemed ludicrous. "You don't think it's too farfetched to believe that Phil would go to that extreme? I mean, think about the specifics—locating the car service Kurt uses, finding out where they would be at any given time, and then actually getting away with tampering without anyone being the wiser. I just don't see it. Maybe it was an accident."

"Other things fit, though," Laurel pointed out, sharing a look with Smith. The two of them had both been personally involved in this investigation, so they had stake in how this ended. "Who else knows how to take down a security system? The regular Joe Schmoe doesn't, but someone with Phil's kind of expert knowledge? And to top it off, he had access to the office building after hours."

"We all agree the person who killed Brad most likely works at Manon Investments, but we're leaving out the other people in the building." Grace took another bite of her pizza before wiping her fingers on the napkin in her lap. "There are a lot of offices with a lot of employees. It's possible that Brad upset some connected guys he shouldn't have been borrowing money from, and just maybe his death had nothing to do with Kurt Langston, Phil Colbert, or the firm."

Everyone began to put in their two cents in on if Phil had anything to do with Brad's murder. They debated on whether or not the man was able to kill someone in cold blood, and then took the conversation in another direction that included the possibility that maybe Kurt Langston hired some wise guy to do the job.

"It doesn't make sense," Cynthia said to Gareth, keeping this particular conversation between the two of them. "There was no need for Kurt to kill Brad. None at all."

"I agree, but it does seem strangely coincidental that all of this came out now."

"Meredith?" Cynthia tossed the name out there, because the woman always seemed to be involved in some way. "She was the one to bring the letter to everyone's attention. Brad had a home office, so it's not surprising that he would have kept some of his more personal files there."

"Meredith was also having an affair with Steve," Gareth

pointed out, polishing off his pizza while giving a sideways glance to the paper plate still in her hand. "One breadstick? Really?"

Cynthia took another bite, not having touched her glass of wine since the food arrived. Gareth was right. She shouldn't drink on an empty stomach.

"You realize that this brings some items on the agenda closed in relation to Langston." Another round of laughter went around the room at something Rye said, but neither Cynthia or Gareth joined in on that side of the conversation. "Think about it. The police were able to question Langston before his accident, Phil Colbert was forced to come clean about his illegal actions and subsequently fired, and the firm is basically now in Smith's hands."

Cynthia hadn't thought of it like that, but Gareth had a point. Yes, some dirty plays had taken place, but the decks had been cleaned. Tomorrow dawned a new day, and so far it appeared relatively normal.

Her appetite began to come back, and she even tossed Gareth a smile.

"You're right." Cynthia then began to consider the upside to today's events. "Don't get me wrong, I do feel bad about the accident involving Kurt and his poor driver. No matter what my feelings are about the situation, no one should suffer through something like that. But Smith was able to control the narrative, I didn't have to publicly humiliate myself in front of the financial industry, and the police most likely have more information that could help them solve Brad's murder."

"And that means tomorrow will be like any other day. Well, the days before this whole thing blew up."

Gareth smiled at seeing Cynthia regaining her ability to eat. She couldn't help but return his silly grin, because this was the first time since Brad's murder that she experienced a sense of normalcy.

Her sordid past was out in the open, his past had been laid bare, and they were still standing…together. Yes, Brad's killer was still in the wind, but everyone she cared for seemed to be out of that individual's crosshairs and out from under police suspicion.

Excitement for what the future held for them blossomed, and she impulsively leaned into him and pressed her lips against his. The worst of times were behind them, and their future was trimmed with gold.

"I know this is probably the worst place to do this, but I need you to know that I love you, Gareth Nicollet," Cynthia whispered, pulling away just far enough to observe his reaction. She smiled even more when those gold flecks shimmered in his eyes. "And for the record? I've never said those three words to another man…ever."

"Think we can leave this little get-together a bit early?" Gareth's gaze held a promise that she might be a bit tired come morning. "I'd like to continue this conversation back at the hotel."

"About that…" Cynthia allowed her voice to trail off as she realized she never had a chance to tell him that she'd checked him out of the hotel this morning. The key she'd made for him was still in the side pocket of her purse. "Let's go to my place tonight. There's something I want to—"

Another round of laughter went around the room, preventing Cynthia from revealing anything else too soon. She slowly lowered her plate. It wasn't hard to miss the curious stare Gareth was leveling her, but time was now on their side.

"…looked beautiful," Smith said as the group had clearly veered away from the subject of murder and mayhem. He only had eyes for Laurel at the moment. "The charity dinner was a huge success."

"And an added bonus was the fact that I made it through dinner without spilling anything on the white linen tablecloths." Laurel wiped her lips with her napkin before setting it on top of her empty paper plate. She scrunched one side of her mouth to the side before adding more thoughts on the evening she'd spent weeks getting ready for. "Detective Nielsen was there, but he wasn't very forthcoming on the investigation. Of course, that was all before Kurt Langston showed up at Cynthia's apartment."

"It wasn't the time to talk business, either." Smith took her plate and piled it on top of his, not missing the sideways glare Laurel aimed in his direction. "I'm just saying that—"

"It wasn't like I bombarded him with questions. As a matter of fact, someone else brought it up while we were all mingling, and it seemed like the perfect opportunity for me to put my two cents into the conversation." Laurel shot a knowing smile to both Cynthia and Grace. "We didn't get where we are today by sitting on the sidelines."

"Here, here," Cynthia said, not bothering to hide her satisfaction behind the rim of her wineglass. Laurel was right, and there were times that they all needed to step up to the plate. They'd all done so professionally, but it was time she solidified her personal life. She drained the rest of her wine, noting that it was a good thing she polished off those breadsticks. "Listen, everyone. It's been a hell of a day. Gareth and I are going to call it a night."

It didn't take long for everyone to agree about the kind of day they'd all been through, and her words had been the catalyst to bring this evening to a close. Cynthia always thought of herself as well composed, but she couldn't tamp down her excitement about what was still to come.

"We're going to need to stop by the hotel so that I can grab a few items." They were roughly a few feet from her vehicle, and the snow flurries were still sporadic. That didn't mean the bitter wind hadn't picked up, almost as if Mother Nature was warning them about the coming winter season. Cynthia tried not to take that as a sign for the rest of the evening, but there was absolutely no way she was going to convince Gareth to drive straight to her apartment without a good reason. "The temperature is dropping, though. Road are becoming somewhat slick. Maybe we should—"

"Gareth, I checked you out of the hotel this morning," Cynthia said abruptly, turning up the collar on her dress coat before bringing him to a stop right before he reached for the handle on the passenger door. She needed to observe his reaction, because her mother had always said that mental pictures were worth more than any Polaroid. "We've been seeing each other for over eight months. I think it's time for us to…"

It was rare that Cynthia misread a situation, but it was clear by the expression on his face that she'd overstepped her bounds. Technically, his bounds. This wasn't how tonight was supposed to go. She should have had another glass of wine to take the edge off, because the look of surprise that crossed his features caused her entire body to go numb.

Her reaction had nothing to do with the cold temperatures. She took a step back, doing her best to regain her composure. Her mother's advice had backfired, and now she would forever remember this moment.

Unfortunately, it was impossible to rip those mental photographs into shreds.

CHAPTER THIRTEEN

"**D**ON'T." GARETH HADN'T meant for Cynthia to take his temporary shock at hearing those words the wrong way, but it was clear she now assumed she'd taken things too fast. He stepped forward to close the distance she'd put between them. "Cyn, you—"

"It's clear I misread the situation." Cynthia tilted her chin, her blue eyes appearing colder than the wind chill. She was so quick to react. God, he loved her fire. "You can—"

Gareth kissed her, right there in the middle of the sidewalk underneath the streetlight with snow flurries falling around them. He didn't care that the agents Rye had hired to keep an eye on Grace were more than likely getting a show. There was no use worrying about outward appearances if he couldn't convince her that his reaction was anything but negative.

Her lips were warm. He planned on making them burn. It took her only seconds to respond. She tasted of the wine she'd been sipping on, and he wanted more.

He wanted all of her in this instance in time and forever more.

The kiss went on until neither one of them could breathe, and even then the condensation from their exhalations merged together as one.

"You caught me by surprise, Cyn. That's all it was." Gareth wrapped a hand around the back her of neck, wanting her close until she'd heard every word he had to say to her proposal. "I want nothing more than to spend my life with you. You're my soulmate. I've spent every spare minute I've had these past eight months in this bitter cold city with only the idea of you to keep me warm, all because this is where you decided to live. In case you hadn't noticed, I'd follow you all the way to Antarctica if need be."

"But you—"

"Needed to make sure I heard you correctly," Gareth quickly amended her, not willing to make the same mistake twice. "A lot has been thrown at you…at both of us…in this last month. Cyn, you are everything I've ever wanted, and I couldn't possibly ask for anything more. Nothing on earth nor anyone on its face could take me from you now."

Gareth kissed her once more before seeing her safely inside her vehicle. She had one of those self-starters that he'd activated before leaving Rye's residence, so the inside was nice and warm. He quickly joined her, but neither one of them said another word until he'd pulled into her parking garage.

"You really checked me out of my hotel?" Gareth opened the driver's side door, though he waited for her to respond.

Her smile said it all.

"Would it help to know that I gave you a quarter of my walk-in closet?"

"I bet that hurt more than you thought it would," Gareth said with a laugh, wanting nothing more than to have them make it to her apartment before they began to lose particles of clothing. "Maybe we should consider something a bit larger than your small one bedroom apartment."

"You read my mind," Cynthia murmured, taking him by the tie and pulling him close. He had no choice but to pull the door shut, closing them inside the still warm vehicle. "Did you know that this seat goes all the way back?"

She'd removed her dress coat when they were halfway home, so she had no trouble climbing over the console and proving to him that the driver's seat really did fold all the way down.

"Cyn, I'm well aware that we both like pushing the limits, but—"

"No one can see us in the corner here," Cyn whispered, leaning over him until she'd wrapped her hands around the metal components of the headrest. "And I can't wait until we reach that distant apartment. That's too far, and I want you now. I need you, Gareth."

Cynthia had pushed her pencil skirt up around her hips before she'd been able to straddle him. Honestly, he'd been hard ever since they'd kissed outside on the sidewalk. Not even the cold temperatures outside could ruin this moment.

"Then take what you want of me, Cyn."

Cynthia released her hold on the headrest before pushing herself up so that she had free access to his belt. Her hair cascaded down her cheeks as she focused on the task at hand, giving him time to admire her beauty.

Eight months.

He needed an eternity with her.

"Marry me."

Her laughter bubbled as her fingers fumbled. When he purposefully didn't crack a smile, she stopped what she was doing and stared at him with those blue eyes so filled with shock—the same disbelief he'd experienced when she'd all but stated that she wanted him to live with her.

"We're a little unorthodox, aren't we?" Gareth asked softly, reaching up and tucking the right side of her hair behind her ear. "I don't want to waste even a second, Cyn. I want to know that you'll wear my ring and walk by my side hand in hand. Allow me the honor of growing old together with you. Will you become my wife, Cynthia Marie Ellsworth?"

"Yes."

Cynthia would have said more, but there was no need. Anything either of them had to say could wait until they celebrated in the most unconventional way. He pulled her down until he could capture her lips, deciding to take matters into his own hands.

It didn't take him long to unfasten his dress pants, release his cock from the confines of his briefs, and roll on the condom she'd help take out of his wallet.

"Yes." Cynthia repeated the word, though he was relatively sure the exclamation now held a double meaning. Her warmth surrounded him as she took his cock inside of her. This position allowed her to take every inch of him until their moans mingled into one. "Yes."

The windows had begun to fog over, and their body heat was enough to keep the inside of the vehicle warm. Anyone walking by wouldn't have to guess as to what was taking place inside the BMW Coupe.

Their presence inside was patently obvious.

Gareth pressed his lips against her neck, relishing the movement of her hips as she continued to rotate in small circles. She was taking her pleasure, and he was more than willing to give in to his.

Her sweet fragrance surrounded him, and he struggled to allow her the ability to control the pace of their union. The promise of such a bright future ahead of them had him wanting to pound into her over and over, staking his claim. It was a primitive reaction that he could barely control.

Cynthia finally began to quicken the pace, but she was still gyrating and rubbing her clit while keeping him on the edge. He lightly bit the cord of her neck before digging his fingers into her hips, letting her know that he only had so much patience left.

"Take what you need, Cyn," Gareth encouraged her through his clenched teeth. She was basically killing him, but he'd let her in this moment. He was hers to do with as she pleased. He wasn't surprised when she began to use her knees as leverage, pulling her off of him before taking him back to her core. "That's right. I'm yours, Cyn. Heart, mind, and soul."

Cynthia sat up so that she could rest one hand on the roof of the vehicle and the other on his chest. He steadied her with his grip and prayed that he had the ability to stop his need to complete the act. She was hell on his control.

The warm walls of her sheath began to tighten around his cock, initiating a burning need to meet her halfway. She quickened her pace even more until he was positive the vehicle was bouncing in time with their movements. He recognized the moment she hit that sweet precipice from the way she cried out his name.

Gareth didn't hold back either, now taking full control and using his grip on her pelvis to drive into her over and over again. He didn't stop until she was lying on top of him, both of them struggling for air.

"Okay," Cynthia breathed out, managing to take in enough oxygen to finish her thought. "I can move some of my shoes to the guest closet. That should give you another set of cubbies in the walk-in closet, but no more."

Gareth pressed a kiss to her temple, always appreciative of Cynthia's witty replies when she was overcome with emotion. Well, that made two of them. He couldn't wait to get started on their future.

"I guess we'll have to start looking at houses then."

CHAPTER FOURTEEN

"IT'S A RATHER extensive skin care regime." Cynthia protested by giving him a shove to the side with her shoulder. She saw the way Gareth had been staring at the numerous bottles on the bathroom counter. "And if you say one word about it, you'll find that you've lost that extra section in the closet."

The golden flecks in his eyes practically glowed with laughter as he pulled her in front of him, not caring that she was wearing nothing but a towel with water droplets still on her shoulders. It was a wonder they were both able to function this morning. They might have gotten two whole hours of sleep.

He'd let her catch another thirty minutes of slumber while he took a shower, but then he woke her in the most spectacular manner. Her knees barely had enough strength remaining to keep her upright in the shower, but she'd managed with the promise of a tall glass of orange juice…which was sitting on the corner of the counter. It promised the energy to carry on.

"Cyn, you can have the entire closet if it means I get to spend the rest of my life with you." Gareth pressed his lips inside the curve of her neck. She immediately closed her eyes at the sensual stimulation he initiated with the stroke of his tongue as he licked away some of the water. "Hmmmm. You make me want to take the day off so that we can make further plans."

"Like?" Cynthia asked, her thoughts immediately conjuring up the two of them in bed with their legs entwined. "We never did get to try—"

The light pinch on her ass had her spinning around with laughter, but he caught her before she could pull away.

"Get your mind out of bed for more than a minute, woman," Gareth said with false indignation. The smile on his handsome face said it all, but he'd awakened her sexual goddess once again. He wasn't going to get to make a clean getaway that easy. "On a serious note, I want you to take a few days from work so that you can meet my parents. My siblings can wait another week or two. I don't want you running for the hills quite yet."

Speaking of running, they hadn't been taking their daily runs. There had been no time in their schedules, but they'd have to change that. Unless they were going to start substituting their workout routine with a new one.

Oh, yes. This relationship was definitely moving to the next level.

"Does next week work?"

Cynthia didn't hesitate, never surer of anything in her life. She wrapped her arms around his neck, grateful that she didn't have to worry about too much height difference. They were perfect for each other in nearly every way she could imagine. She didn't want to waste another day, but this did call for an afternoon of shopping with Laurel and Grace.

"I'll set it up with my people," Gareth murmured against her lips, kissing her like he never had any intention of letting her get ready for the day. He didn't pull away until once again her knees began to tremble. "Mint. I like it."

"You know, we can always—"

"I have that overseas call regarding the reconstruction of that desalination plant in Yemen," Gareth said rather regretfully. He smoothed back her wet strands before ending this moment of bliss with a soft kiss to her forehead. She closed her eyes and savored his gentleness, taking that mental picture her mother had always told her to take in moments like these. "I'll go make you a protein shake to get you started. I don't know if you've had time to look outside, but two inches of snow fell while we were in bed. No running today. We need a decent gym with an indoor track."

Cynthia wondered what she might have done that could remotely have given him the impression that she had enough strength to walk, let alone run after their sexual activities this morning. His faith in her was astonishing.

"I think I burned all the calories I needed to for the day," Cynthia quipped, managing to get a nice tap on his rear end for good measure after he'd turned to walk out of the bathroom. She continued to watch his subtle swagger as he crossed the threshold. "I could so get used to this."

"I heard that, and I'm in full agreement."

Cynthia spent the next forty-five minutes doing her morning routine, choosing a black business suit with her one of her favorite burgundy blouses and matching heels. She did hesitate for just a moment in front of her shoe rack after spotting the pair of black heels that had offered her a string of good luck.

A quick glance in the mirror changed her mind. Even she could perceive the glow that surrounded her after such a magical night. She wasn't usually the romantic type, per se. It was time to move forward though, and not get hung up on her past.

"I can still kiss you, right?" Gareth asked when she walked into the kitchen, his gaze landing on the matching lipstick she'd chosen specifically to wear with this blouse. "Otherwise, you're going to have to reapply quite often today."

"Test it out," Cynthia encouraged enticingly, closing the distance between them and tilting her head to offer him her lips.

She'd purposefully chosen the brand that stayed on during day, even through meals. "You can kiss me all you want, Mr. Nicollet."

They managed to get out of the apartment fifteen minutes later, though Cynthia did have to take her strawberry protein shake with her in the car. Gareth drove, though he did have to adjust the driver's seat back into position after their little diversion last night. They were both still smiling when he finally pulled into the parking garage of her work building.

"Lunch?" Gareth asked after they'd entered the elevator. He pressed the correct button, but then leaned forward to place his hand over the sliding doors. "I could make us a reservation at Manny's."

"That sounds wonderful," Cynthia replied, stepping back when she realized that Gareth had seen Marilyn walking toward the elevator. "Good morning, Marilyn."

"It hasn't been as good as I'd hoped." Marilyn was wearing a pair of winter boots and a heavy winter jacket, which she was currently brushing off with a gloved hand. "My car wouldn't start, and I had to call a car service. Now I'm late, and Paul and Smith have that meeting with their lawyers to go over the transition."

"I'm sure it will be fine," Gareth assured her, stepping closer to Cynthia to make room for Marilyn. The doors slid quietly closed, leaving the overhead music to waft softly over them in an attempt to ease their stress. It sure wasn't working for Marilyn. "I spoke with Smith this morning. He mentioned the meeting wasn't until one o'clock, so you'll have plenty of time to get the conference room ready."

"Yes, but Smith mentioned he had a couple of interviews set up for Vern's position later this morning." Marilyn unzipped her coat and then patted the back of her hair to ensure that the sprayed strands hadn't moved. "I wanted to have the coffee machine going and the list of candidates printed off before Smith arrived this morning."

It was sweet that Marilyn wanted to impress the man who was going to be her new boss. With that said, the woman had been here longer than any of them, with the exception of Paul. She had nothing to worry about. This place couldn't function without her.

The loud chime drowning out the music signaled they'd arrived at their floor. The elevator traffic was rarely busy this early in the morning. The other businesses didn't roll in until eight o'clock, whereas the financial firms were mostly in the office around seven in the morning due to the market hours being on Eastern Standard Time (EST).

"Hey," Gareth said to Cynthia softly, allowing Marilyn to zip through the glass doors as if her life depended on it. "Noon for lunch. Don't forget."

Cynthia's burgundy heels were rather high, so all she had to do was lean forward so that their lips were touching. She was conscious of who was milling around in the office. Not that it mattered. Everyone was well aware of her relationship with Gareth now, and they also understood that she would never allow her personal life to interfere with her career.

"It's a date," Cynthia promised, knowing she'd have to make time for a quick shopping spree with Laurel and Grace later on in the week. "Don't work too hard."

"Ditto."

Cynthia breezed through the glass doors after Marilyn, though the older woman was nowhere to be found. The usual soothing smell of leather, paper, and coffee filled the air. Someone had beat Marilyn to the coffee maker. Of course, nothing could erase the scent of Gareth's cologne that had rubbed off onto the collar of her coat.

She made it to her office, where she took the time to hang up her dress coat on the antique rack she'd bought in Stillwater. She hadn't needed to wear her winter boots today, thanks to the numerous skyways of the city. She always kept her spare set was in the back of her vehicle in case of emergencies, anyway.

The ringing of her desk phone told her the day was about to get started. A quick look at the base told her that it was an interoffice call.

"Good morning," Laurel said, obviously having had her coffee. "Smith spoke with Detective Nielsen this morning to get an update on the investigation. It looks as if there's no change on Kurt Langston's condition. I thought you'd like to know in regard to the case, at least."

"Give me a minute. I'll grab Grace and walk down in your direction."

Cynthia hung up the phone and then grabbed her strawberry protein shake she'd set on her desk. She hadn't even reached her office door before Grace appeared with a big smile on her face. It appeared that she had a fantastic evening, as well.

"Pearls."

The one word had Cynthia instantly reaching for her necklace. She hadn't consciously realized she'd worn them today, but it wasn't much of a surprise. She would always equate these beautiful pearls with Gareth.

"Pearls," Cynthia agreed with a knowing smile, knowing that said it all. "Did you hear that—"

"Shoot," Grace muttered, having glanced into the trading room as they were walking through the foyer. "Give me a minute. I need to speak with Steve about that option trade he executed."

Grace veered off to the right, leaving Cynthia to continue

towards Laurel's office. Marilyn wasn't at her desk, but that wasn't surprising given what she said about all the meetings this morning. Needless to say, the last thing Cynthia expected was to see Marilyn coming out of Brad's office down at the end of the corridor.

"Excuse me, ma'am?"

Cynthia was brought up short by who she assumed was someone here for the interviews Smith was conducting, though she was rather distracted at the moment by what was taking place in front of her. It was clear that Marilyn was a bit taken aback, but she straightened her shoulders as she continued to walk forward.

What the hell had she been doing in Brad's office? No one at the firm had gone into his domain at the end of the corridor since the murder. At least, not that she knew of.

"Can I help you?" Cynthia asked, normally not in this position to greet guests. "I assume you're here to meet with Smith Gallo?"

Cynthia pasted a smile on her lips, all the while keeping an eye on Marilyn.

"Yes, I have an interview with him this morning. My name is Cade Makin." The man held out his hand, leaving her no choice but to return his greeting. "Mr. Gallo is aware of my work situation and told me to come in early to allow me to facilitate that need."

"Of course. It's nice to meet you." Cynthia released his hand before gesturing toward Marilyn, who was quickly closing the distance between them. "I'm going to leave you in Marilyn's capable hands."

Cynthia was able to excuse herself, but not before she requested to speak with Marilyn the first chance she had. The woman acknowledged the bid before escorting Cade Makin over to the small waiting area back in front at reception.

What the hell was going on here?

Cynthia would have gone straight into the guest office, but the door was already closed. Gareth had mentioned an important conference call earlier. She didn't want to bother him, but this wasn't something she could keep to herself.

"Laurel, did you see that?" Cynthia asked, quickly closing the door behind her. "I just saw Marilyn coming out of Brad's office."

"I know," Laurel confessed with a disgusted expression crossing her pretty features. "I still have trouble walking down the damn hallway, let alone actually opening his door. I don't care if the cleaning crew took care of…well, every possible thing in there. All I see is blood."

Cynthia took the guest chair, noticing that the protein shake she had yesterday was still sitting on Laurel's desk.

"Don't even think about leaving without taking that disgusting drink out of here with you." Laurel picked up her disposable coffee cup from the café downstairs before leaning back in her chair. "I'd meant to throw it away, but I don't want the smell in my trashcan."

"Laurel, I'm obviously missing something." Cynthia's fingers were starting to become cold from carrying around the drink Gareth had made her before leaving the apartment. She set it down beside the other one, ignoring Laurel's arched eyebrow. "Why is Marilyn using Brad's office?"

"Oh, that." Laurel dismissed Cynthia's concern with a wave of her hand. "Marilyn needed to make a private call yesterday. With Gareth using the guest office, she thought no one would mind if she used Brad's office. She—"

Laurel's lips formed a perfect O as she quickly leaned forward, splashing a bit of coffee on her desk. It was finally sinking in how odd it was for Marilyn to enter the domain where a murder had taken place, and one that had her in tears not four weeks ago.

"Sorry about that. Steve can be such an ass some—" Grace broke off her tirade about the trader, coming to a stop upon seeing Laurel's dubious expression. "What happened? What did I miss?"

"Let me ask you a question first," Cynthia said in the lowest voice possible. Her adrenaline had begun pumping, and the palms of her hands started to perspire. What if they were right? "Do you think Marilyn is capable of cold-blooded murder?"

CHAPTER FIFTEEN

"I WAS HOPING you'd still be in town."

To say Gareth was surprised that Meredith Manon had sought him out in the same office space where her ex-husband had been murdered was an understatement. This was the second time he'd seen her in two days, which was a hell of a lot more than he'd had the pleasure of her company in the last two years. He quietly set his pen down on the papers he'd been reviewing while quickly going through a list of reasons she could possibly want with him.

"Meredith," Gareth greeted before indicating she should take a seat. "I fly back out on Friday."

Gareth didn't feel any need to explain to her that he would be in Minneapolis a lot more in the coming weeks, months, and years. It honestly didn't matter that he intended to make this city his home base. He and Meredith were mere acquaintances at this point.

"What exactly can I do for you?"

He steeled himself against the usual request, having gotten used to the appeals for money. Brad had a lot of debt acquired at the time of his death, not that he'd shared that information with Gareth. They hadn't really been on great speaking terms toward the end.

"I found some pictures going through Brad's things that I thought you'd like to have," Meredith replied tentatively before reaching into her purse and pulling out a couple of photographs. "They must have been taken at the hospital the day you were born."

Gareth didn't like to be taken off guard. This moment definitely qualified in that arena, but he leaned forward to take the pictures from her anyway. He'd come to terms with his childhood and adoption long ago. This didn't change anything. Why, then, did something about this offering feel off?

"I appreciate you bringing these to me." Gareth wasn't about to look at something so personal with someone looking on that he had no connection with. He set them down alongside his pen before carrying on the conversation so that this visit didn't become any more awkward than it already was. "I know that you and Brad had remained friends after your divorce. I'm sure it's not easy going through his personal items."

"I've been finding out a lot about Brad that I'd wished I'd known when we were married." Meredith's wistful expression caught him off guard. He'd heard about her affair with Steve Lewis. She'd obviously gotten over the embarrassment of it all. The divorce had been years ago, and both she and Brad had moved on with their lives. This was a development Gareth hadn't seen coming. "Did you know that he still kept our wedding picture in his wallet? Or that he gave me the house when his lawyer had advised against it?"

Gareth didn't know any of that, though he was aware that Brad had still been paying on the mortgage. His life insurance policy had barely been enough to pay it off, though Meredith had acquired some shares in Manon Investments. It wasn't a lot in the grand scheme of things, but it wasn't like Meredith relied on any income Brad had been giving her since their divorce. She'd carved out a life for herself, and it seemed to be going pretty well for her.

"I think it's safe to say that he never stopped caring for you, Meredith." Gareth thought back to when he'd found out that she'd been having an affair with Steve Lewis. It shouldn't have made a difference, seeing as Meredith and Brad hadn't been married for quite some time. But it did take some type of odd courage to sleep with a colleague of her ex-husband. "You know that Brad and I didn't have the closest of relationships, but what happened was a tragedy for us all."

"I remember when you reached out to Brad's mother," Meredith recalled with a fond smile that Gareth found oddly confusing. She hadn't treated him with the most openness of affection. "Brad had conflicting emotions over your return. You do know that he was jealous of you, right? It's the reason he held you at arm's length for all those years."

Well, that solidified it. She was crossing into territory that wasn't any of her damn business. He sure as hell wasn't having this conversation with a woman who had nothing to do with his past, nor anything to do with his future.

"Meredith, Brad and I were related by blood. There was nothing more between us." Gareth pushed back his chair and held his tie against his shirt as he stood, signifying that this visit was over. "I appreciate you bringing me the pictures."

Gareth was relieved that he hadn't told Meredith that he was moving his home base to Minneapolis. Honestly, there was no reason for them to see one another after she left the office today. It wasn't like she had anything to do with Manon Investments, especially considering she'd already had a discussion with Paul to give her shares back to the company.

"Oh. Okay. I didn't mean to keep you." Meredith gave him an apologetic smile, though he doubted she regretted stopping in to see him. He didn't know what game she was playing, but he didn't want any part of it. "I should be getting back to Brad's apartment, anyway. The last of the furniture has been moved to the house, and I'm expecting a cleaning crew in a couple of hours."

Once again, Gareth wasn't sure why Meredith was sharing all of this with him. He walked around the desk and patiently waited for her stand before he walked her to the door. He didn't stop there, either. He escorted her through the foyer.

"Meredith, what are you doing here?"

Both Gareth and Meredith turned at the sound of her name, but not before he caught sight of the confliction crossing her features. It was then he understood the real reason for her visit, and he had nothing to do with it.

"Oh, I was just dropping something off to Gareth," Meredith replied casually, contradicting the fact that she was clutching the strap to her purse. She was now completely facing Steve, waiting for his reaction. When he didn't reply right away, she filled in the silent gap. "How are you?"

"Um, do you have a second?" Steve inquired, scratching the back of his head as if he were unsure of asking her such a question. "I've been meaning to call you, but I think having this discussion in person would be better."

Meredith slowly stepped forward, leaving Gareth standing in the middle of the foyer as he watched the two of them walk into the trading room. It wasn't like they would get a ton of privacy in there, but then again, Gareth wasn't even remotely sure about what he'd just witnessed.

"What was that about?" Cynthia had sidled up next to him, giving her light perfume a chance to surround him.

"I have no earthly clue," Gareth muttered, still trying to figure out if Meredith had used the photographs as an excuse for her to come into the office. "I thought it was Meredith who cut things off with Steve."

"You could say that," Cynthia said somewhat distractedly. "Meredith asked Steve if he killed Brad. It was a pretty big thing, and he was basically crushed. I don't believe they've spoken since that day."

Gareth was a little taken aback by the manner in which she'd just conveyed the events of Steve and Meredith's relationship. Cynthia usually would have interjected her opinion in the middle, but she wasn't even looking in the direction of the trading room anymore.

Her gaze was intently locked on Marilyn.

"I was on the phone for forty minutes," Gareth said wryly. He'd thought this day was a turning point. "What could I have possibly missed in that amount of time?"

"Kurt's condition still remains critical, Smith is conducting interviews for Vern's position, and Marilyn has been using Brad's office to make personal phone calls since you're using the guest office," Cynthia summed it up before flashing him a smile. "How was your overseas conference call?"

"I think I'm going to go make another one." Gareth was well aware that when Cynthia tugged on a string, she got the immense need to unravel the entire sweater. He didn't want to be anywhere near the carnage when she was done figuring out why Marilyn could manage to use Brad's office after having had a crew brought in to clean up all the blood. "Just remember, the woman is in her sixties. It's doubtful she committed murder by herself."

Did Gareth believe that Marilyn slit Brad's throat until he bled out? No, not even for one moment. That wouldn't stop Cynthia from needing to prove that to herself. Her tenacity was one of the reasons he loved her.

"Try to stay out of trouble, Cyn." Gareth didn't care who was watching. He leaned in and stole a kiss. "I know it's not your strong suit."

"Hey, I'm not the one who found my boss dead or got false-ly arrested for his murder," Cynthia reminded him, purposefully leaving out the fact that she could have very well been included in that list had Kurt Langston been the guilty party. "One, I don't do blood. Two, I don't look good in orange. Three, it's part of my job to keep things running smoothly here."

"Uh-huh," Gareth agreed half-heartedly. He stepped to the side when she would have backhanded him softly in the arm. "You keep telling yourself that, sweetheart. I'm getting back to work. Remember, we have a lunch date today at noon."

Cynthia didn't know that Gareth was leaving the office at around eleven o'clock. He'd be back before she even realized he was missing. He had an appointment with one of the best jewelers in the city, fully intending to ask Cynthia for her hand in marriage in the proper manner before he was needed in some far-off corner of Africa.

He'd also have to begin looking for office space locally, because he wouldn't be able to use Manon Investments as a temporary workplace forever. He wasn't going to worry about that now, but it was something to add to his long list of priorities.

Maybe it was time to hire a competent personal assistant—one who was capable of lifting some of the weight without becoming a hindrance.

Gareth returned to the guest office, unable to forget about the photographs Meredith had brought in for him. He had little regret in his life, but his relationship with Brad hadn't been as healthy as it should have in the grand scheme of things.

He chose the first picture, holding the old square photo gently in between his fingers. His biological mother was holding him in her arms, where he was swaddled in a white blanket. She was staring down at him with a mixture of regret and hope. Her expression reassured him that she'd made the right decision for everyone involved.

Gareth instinctively reached for the second photograph.

The image spoke a thousand words.

He slowly sank into the leather of the desk chair, absorbing the fact that Meredith had been right in her assumption of the situation. A young boy could be seen standing in the corner of the hospital room, looking on as Gareth was being handed to a nurse…presumably to be taken to his adopted parents.

The look of yearning on the youthful face was heart wrenching. Brad had to watch on as his infant brother had been given away, escaping a life of the unknown. The Manons had struggled on and off throughout their lives. That was, until Brad had attended college and put everything into his career path.

"You should have been proud of yourself, Brad," Gareth muttered, sitting back in his chair as he continued to stare at the little boy who hadn't gotten to live a full life. "You were taken too soon, before you learned what was truly important in life."

A ball of emotions formed in Gareth's throat at what could have been instead of what had been. If anything, this was a valuable lesson to never take anything for granted.

Gareth made a snap decision, deciding to head to the jewelry store a bit early. He dropped the photograph on the desk before standing and grabbing the keys to Cynthia's vehicle.

Today was the day he was going to make their engagement official.

Today was a new beginning, and an end to regret.

CHAPTER SIXTEEN

"…MAKE A DECISION sometime next week," Paul continued, having been speaking for the last ten minutes about the upcoming changes to the firm. All the employees were gathered around the trading desk, allowing Steve to continue to monitor the day's trades. "Smith has asked me to stay on as CFO of Gallo Capital Management, and I've chosen to accept."

A round of congratulations went around the room, though this wasn't an unexpected announcement. Smith had been pretty upfront with everyone, not allowing any doubt about the future of his new firm.

"Steve has decided to join his brother-in-law in London. As most of you know, Joshua Green will be joining Gallo Capital Management when the switch is official. There will also be considerable positive changes to the benefits package for everyone."

"That must have been what Steve was talking to Meredith about," Grace whispered, holding up her coffee cup to block her voice from carrying too far. "She left here crying."

Laurel and Grace were standing on either side of Cynthia. They'd been listening to Paul for quite a while, and it was evident that Smith was about to step in and finish up the dialogue.

"Meredith has no one else to blame but herself," Laurel said softly, shaking her head at the fact that the woman had all but accused her own lover of murder. "That relationship was doomed from the very start."

"Speaking of relationships, you and Gareth seem to have overcome that former hurdle that had been in the way," Laurel murmured, a knowing smile on her lips as her eyes drifted down to the pearls strung around Cynthia's neck. "I like this new transition for us. Any bets on which one of us gets married first?"

Grace nearly choked on her coffee, garnering stares from the other employees around them.

"Looks like you might be in trouble, Laurel." Cynthia let her gaze drift to the front of the room where Smith was raising an eyebrow their way. His displeasure was evident, and Cynthia couldn't blame him. It wasn't polite to talk over the speaker, but then again, Smith had been in enough meetings with Paul to know that these meetings could drag on forever. "Changing the topic here, but I haven't had a chance to speak with Marilyn. She hasn't been at her desk long enough for me to catch her, but I find it really odd that she can go into Brad's office as if he hadn't been found dead at his desk a month ago. She cried for almost a week straight anytime anyone would glance toward his door."

"People handle grief in different ways."

"Or she killed him," Grace interjected with a shrug, having made a full recovery after clearing her airway.

"Prison made you a hard bitch," Cynthia replied with a smile, though nothing about this situation was humorous. "You were right, Laurel. We're all going to hell in a handbag."

They all quieted down when Smith took over the meeting, hopefully to bring it to a close. Cynthia had some work matters to tie up before she went to lunch with Gareth, who seemed to have disappeared from the office earlier. She glanced at her watch. They were supposed to meet in the foyer a few minutes before noon, so she still had forty-five minutes to spare.

The vibration of her cell phone that she'd been holding told her that she had an incoming call, but a quick glance at the display revealed an unknown number. She debated answering, but she figured it best she take the call given that so much had occurred over the last couple of days. Turning toward the back of the room to be less of a distraction, she accepted the call.

"Hello?" Cynthia rested a finger against her other ear as she quietly took a few steps farther away from the meeting. The man on the other end of the line all but verified this call wasn't going to be good. She walked as far as the foyer before her heart began to beat once more. "Detective Nielsen. Has something happened?"

Cynthia closed her eyes, as if that was going to stop the detective from telling her that Kurt had either died or had woken up with some horrible confession that could potentially ruin her career.

"Would it be possible for you to come to the hospital? The doctor has just been in to speak with Mrs. Langston, and it appears that her husband has awakened." The detective's long pause didn't sooth Cynthia's anxiety that the day wasn't going to go as well as she'd hoped. "I know this is awkward, but Kurt Langston is asking to speak with you, Ms. Ellsworth."

Damn it. She should have worn those black heels.

Cynthia rested a hand over her stomach, trying to ward off the waves of nausea that this call had initiated from the second she'd answered. This wasn't the most ideal diet, but she didn't doubt she'd lost a pound or two over the course of the last month.

"I'll be right there," Cynthia assured him, wishing Gareth were here to accompany her on the drive. "Where should I meet you once I arrive?"

Detective Nielsen explained that Kurt was still in ICU, so she should wait in the hallway until he could get her entry cleared by the doctor. She had a feeling that he meant Kurt's wife, but Cynthia would have to worry about that complication later.

Right now, she needed to figure out a way to the hospital. Gareth had taken her car for whatever meeting he'd had this morning, and a quick unanswered phone call to him told her that either he was out of range or unable to talk right at this moment.

"Is everything okay?" Marilyn asked, seemingly having appeared out of nowhere. "You're looking a bit pale, Cynthia."

Cynthia glanced toward the hallway that led to Brad's corner office, wondering if Marilyn had once again been using the space for personal reasons.

"I'm not entirely sure," Cynthia responded honestly, deciding that the morning was like an episode of "The Twilight Zone". It was best to be direct. That way, her imagination didn't run overtime. "Marilyn, what have you been doing in Brad's office?"

At first, Cynthia's reaction was to back away. There was a glimmer of resentment in the woman's gaze, as well as irritation. Cynthia shot a glance toward the trading room, knowing full well she could scream at the top of her lungs if she was to be stabbed right there in the foyer.

Had Grace been right about Marilyn being able to commit murder? It was what they were all thinking today.

Cynthia's urge to call for help proved unnecessary when the older woman scrunched her nose in defeat, as if the secret of what she'd been doing had been too heavy to keep carrying around. Fortunately, the cloak and dagger behavior was easily explained away.

When had Cynthia become one of those overly dramatic

women?

"I thought I was being so discreet," Marilyn complained, urging Cynthia to follow her down the hallway. She didn't move from her spot in the foyer. "You see, with the company switching names and with Smith taking over as portfolio manager, I thought ordering new business cards would—"

"I'm sure Smith will love what you've done for him, Marilyn."

Cynthia had heard enough to know that she'd been completely wrong about Marilyn hiding some horrible secret. Unfortunately, she'd had taken an innocent act and spiraled it out of control. That alone told her that she was overreacting to the simplest of things.

Honestly, she should have braved the weather and gone for a quick jog this morning. A bit of snow and cold wouldn't have hurt her, and the exercise would have leveled out her emotions.

"You thought that I…"

Marilyn's voice faded, but in such a hurt manner that it caused Cynthia to feel like shit. She was lower than dirt, and there wasn't a thing she could say to make things better. That didn't mean she wasn't going to try.

"I'm sorry, Marilyn. It's only because I found it odd that you were using Brad's office when I know how much his death affected you," Cynthia tried to reason, only ending up making things worse. She couldn't blame her. How else was one supposed to act when basically being accused of murder? "I shouldn't have made assumptions."

"Isn't that what we're all doing, Cynthia?" Marilyn said rather mournfully as she pointed out the flaws of every employee at the firm. She made her way around the large reception area to her chair, though she didn't sit down. "Paul thinks Steve killed Brad, Steve's all but accused Josh of being the killer, Blair thought that Vern had something to do with the murder, and Vern left here muttering that there was no way Phil couldn't be the guilty party. It was easy to see that Detective Mancini thought Smith was responsible, but Detective Nielsen had no choice but to arrest Grace after evidence was planted in her vehicle. And let's not forget Brad's gambling debts."

Cynthia almost sighed with relief that she and Gareth hadn't been included in that list of suspects, but she caught herself just in time. Marilyn wasn't even close to being finished.

Hadn't Cynthia and the others agreed that Marilyn was the backbone of this company? She was like a hard drive that had accumulated a wealth of information over the years.

"Then there's Meredith. I've tried being there for her, but she got too caught up in her affair with Steve. The poor woman doesn't know what she wants. She's lucky that there was enough money for the house to be paid off." Marilyn rested the back of her hand against her forehead, as if assigning motive to each individual was tasking. "And I've known Gareth was Brad's biological brother for many years, so don't think he wasn't the first one I named when the police asked me for my opinion. I'm not saying he could do something that horrible, but those shows on television always have the killer being someone we least suspect."

Cynthia bit her tongue to keep from lashing out at Marilyn for even considering that Gareth could murder anyone, let alone his biological brother. But that would waste too much time, especially when her presence was being requested elsewhere.

She wanted to bring up Kurt Langston. Unfortunately, that meant dragging herself through the mud. But didn't Kurt have the most reason to kill Brad, especially given his role in Phil's deceit?

What were they all missing?

"Marilyn, I'm going to be out of the office for about an hour." Cynthia brought this conversation to a close, otherwise both of them would be here until the end of the day. A quick glance showed that Smith was still taking questions about the transition. "I'll have my cell phone should anyone need me."

Cynthia quickly retrieved her purse, having sent a few text messages so that Laurel and Grace knew why she'd left the office. She also tried calling Gareth again, but he didn't answer. She waited for the beep before giving a brief explanation as to where she was going, and that she would meet him at the restaurant at noon.

It didn't take her long to hail a taxi, hating that she didn't have her car. It was a topic of discussion she needed to have with Gareth, especially since he'd made the decision to make Minneapolis his home base. Yes, he traveled quite a bit, but having a vehicle at his disposal was necessary.

"The hospital, please," Cynthia directed the driver, having closed the door and settled in before the outside temperature could invade the warmth of the cab. It was a good thing the building had the sidewalks cleared or else she would have most likely slipped on the ice in these heels. "And once we get there, please wait for me. I shouldn't be long."

Cynthia sent Gareth a text with the new plans, even though she'd left him a voicemail. Chances were he'd read it before he had a moment to listen to his messages.

She then looked out the window as the taxi pulled away from the curb, joining the rest of the lunch hour traffic. The nausea she'd been able to ward off from earlier returned with a vengeance. She couldn't help but replay Marilyn's ominous words about the guilty party being someone any of them would least suspect.

Cynthia had been focused on Kurt and Phil, but what if a

business transaction had turned personal? What if Kurt's wife realized what was going on with his struggling tech company and had somehow discovered that her husband wasn't as upstanding as she'd once thought.

What if Kurt's wife learned of the affair?

Was Cynthia entering a trap set by Jane Langston?

CHAPTER SEVENTEEN

G ARETH COULDN'T HELP but stare a little longer at the vintage wedding ring—a classic French Belle Époque. The natural pearl was magnificent with some light pink reflects surrounded by old mine cut diamonds set in platinum. The gorgeous specimen resembled a stylized flower circa 1910 Asprey & Garrard Limited.

The ring was rumored to have been commissioned as an anniversary gift from King Edward VII to his wife Alexandra of Denmark just prior to his untimely death in May of 1910. The beautiful gems were elegant yet simple…a portent of understated elegance and truly perfect for the woman he loved.

The exclusivity of Edwardian era jewelry might seem antiquated now and its setting uncomplicated, but as it did in its time…the ring signified Cynthia's uniqueness.

An excitement unlike anything he'd ever experienced overwhelmed him in this moment.

"Sir?" The man behind the counter was holding out his hand so that he could place the small square box in one of the store's sophisticated black and white bags. "I think your future fiancée will be very happy with her very own piece of history."

Gareth gently closed the box before giving it back to the salesman, having already expressed his gratitude to the man who'd acquired such a lovely symbol of love from Sotheby's. He reached into the pocket of his dress coat to pull out his phone, the need arising to hear Cynthia's voice.

Damn it.

He must have left his phone in the console of her vehicle.

"Here you are, sir. We wish you and your future wife the best of luck. It is certainly the best we have to offer and deserving of a good home."

It didn't take long for Gareth to get back to Cynthia's vehicle. He was mindful of the slick spots on the sidewalk, and he took care crossing the street to where he'd parked the car. There had been enough foot traffic to pack down the snow. It was slick if one didn't watch where he or she was stepping. The sky had cast a greyish hue to the day, indicating more snow was in their future.

He didn't mind the cold. Not at all, especially when he was able to spend his nights in bed beside Cynthia.

Gareth pressed the button on the key fob and quickly folded his frame into the driver's seat. He started the engine before reaching for his phone, which was exactly where he'd left it—in the middle of the console. The display showed quite a few missed calls and messages from various business associates, an old friend who wanted to get together for drinks, and Cynthia.

He immediately swiped Cynthia's name to the right, revealing her message that she would meet him at the restaurant after stopping by the hospital to see Kurt Langston.

"What the fuck? Why would she go to see him of all people?" Gareth muttered, wondering why she would do such an out of the ordinary thing. He quickly listened to the voicemail she'd left, hoping that she would shed some light on her crazy decision. When he heard Cynthia explain that Langston had woken up in the ICU and was asking for her, his gaze shot to the digital clock on the dash. "Damn it."

Cynthia most likely had already reached the hospital, but

going to see the man who'd been disloyal to his wife—the same woman who was almost certainly by his bedside—wasn't the best of ideas.

Why would Cynthia go in the first place?

What could possibly have possessed her to make such a decision?

He initiated a call to her, curbing his frustration over the fact that he didn't understand her reasoning. Getting into an altercation with Jane Langston probably wouldn't end well.

After the fifth ring, his call went straight to voicemail. There was no need for him to leave a message, so he hung up and made the decision to drive straight to the restaurant. She'd mentioned that she'd meet him at Manny's, and he trusted her that the situation she found herself in could be resolved peacefully.

Gareth utilized the valet parking at the hotel that the restaurant was located in, taking with him the box he'd removed from the jewelry shop's bag. There wasn't a chance in hell he was leaving something so valuable inside the vehicle unguarded.

He was shown to their table after checking his dress coat, having come to a decision. He then requested a table in the corner for more privacy. There was no need to wait to ask for Cynthia's hand in marriage, and this couldn't have been a more perfect location. The intimate atmosphere was flawless, they'd eaten their first meal together at this restaurant, and this hotel was where they'd first made love.

There were some things that were meant to be—and this was one of them.

"Is there anything I can get for you while you wait for your guest?"

"Coffee, please. Meanwhile, you can let the wine breathe."

Gareth was not surprised to find that Cynthia had yet to

make an appearance. He didn't envy her the inevitable confrontation. Why would Langston have requested to speak with Cynthia to begin with? Had his near-death experience caused him to seek forgiveness?

Ten minutes turned into twenty...with no Cynthia in sight.

Gareth checked his phone for the tenth time, but she hadn't tried to reach him since her last voicemail. He considered himself a patient man, but replaying the question he'd planned on asking her had him craving her presence.

Another five minutes passed, and this time he couldn't stop himself from trying to call her once more.

Voicemail.

She should have answered. She should have already been on her way to the restaurant by now.

Unless something had happened when she'd gone to the hospital...or before she arrived.

Gareth made the hasty decision to abandon the voicemail message and place a call in to the office. Marilyn picked up on the first ring.

"Marilyn, this is Gareth. Is Cynthia still there?"

"I'm sorry, but she stepped out of the office over an hour ago."

"Would you please patch me through to either Laurel or Grace? Whichever one is available," Gareth stipulated abruptly, the two cups of coffee he'd consumed not sitting well in his stomach. Cynthia had been gone for over an hour. As far as he was aware, the ICU was rather strict with the amount of time allowed for visitors. Had she gotten into a confrontation with Jane Langston? "Laurel?"

"Hi, Gareth," Laurel greeted, not sounding concerned in the least. He would have thought her outlook would have eased his concerns, but that was far from the case. "What can I do for you?"

"Have you spoken with Cynthia?"

"Not recently," Laurel replied. "Paul and Smith were conducting a staff meeting, but Cynthia took a phone call in the middle of it. She sent a text saying that Kurt Langston had woken up and wanted to see her. I was honestly surprised that she would go, but she tacked on that she was meeting you for lunch afterward."

Gareth allowed the pause to grow longer as he thought over what could possibly be keeping Cynthia at the hospital. Had Langston's condition reversed? Could he have passed away?

No.

Cynthia would have called him immediately.

"Gareth, what's going on? Why do you sound so concerned?"

"I don't know," Gareth responded honestly, having an urgent need to see Cynthia's beautiful face…right now. "She's not answering her phone, and she should have been here by now. I'm going to head over to the hospital. Listen, if she calls you, please let me know."

Gareth disconnected the call before he lifted a hand to catch the waitress' attention. He'd leave word for Cynthia should she show up at the restaurant. For all he knew, the battery in her cell phone had died…though that was highly unlikely. They had both charged their phones together last night, and he had seventy-three percent charge left on his device.

He quickly relayed the pertinent information before leaving the table and heading toward the front door. They would keep the wine set aside until he returned. Hopefully, he was overreacting and they could both look back at this moment and laugh.

Unfortunately, as much as he'd like to think there was a valid reason for Cynthia not to be answering her phone, an ominous impression told him there was something wrong.

CYNTHIA WASN'T LUCKY enough to have the driver of the cab wait for her near the front entrance of the hospital. She'd have to call for another taxi or car service when she was ready to head to the restaurant.

The sliding doors quietly opened before she stepped into the large foyer. She tilted her head when the strong scent of antiseptic washed over her. This place smelled like every other hospital she'd ever been in. She continued forward until she was standing before the counter of the help desk.

"Excuse me," Cynthia said, catching a woman's attention who was clicking away on her keyboard. "Could you direct me to the ICU?"

Natalie, as her nametag read, pointed Cynthia toward the elevator bank and gave instructions to find the ICU from there. It didn't take her long to arrive at a sterile lobby with a small waiting area outside the large double doors where Detective Nielsen designated they should meet.

She debated removing her winter coat, but she decided against it. It was doubtful that she'd be here long, plus she didn't want to become too exposed. It was silly, really, but the long wool jacket gave her a sense of protection from what was to come.

Cynthia pulled out her cell phone from her purse right as the elevator doors swung open to reveal Detective Nielsen. She'd expected him to come through the ICU doors, but he must have been downstairs grabbing a bite to eat at the cafeteria. At least, she'd deduced that from the stain on his tie. His appearance was a bit ruffled, which was unusual. He was typically well put together and generally didn't have dark circles underneath his eyes.

"Thank you for coming down here, Ms. Ellsworth."

"It was no problem, though I'm not sure why Kurt would want to see me. He—"

The large double doors behind Cynthia swung open, causing her to step aside while a crying woman walked out being comforted by another.

"Detective, was that—"

"Yes," Detective Nielsen replied, his lips compressing in sorrow. He slowly shook his head as he stepped to the side to allow Jane Langston to enter the elevator. "Kurt Langston died around twenty minutes ago."

Cynthia stared in horror and disbelief as the doors slowly slid closed, causing Jane Langston to disappear from view. She'd been crying too hard to even recognize those people around her, and Cynthia was ever grateful that her presence hadn't been noticed.

Kurt Langston had lied and deceived Cynthia into an affair, but Jane Langston most likely wouldn't have cared about the circumstances. She would have instantly accused Cynthia on first sight of having an affair with her husband…who was now dead.

The pain Jane Langston was currently under had to be substantial, and the last thing Cynthia wanted was to add even more.

"I-I don't know what to say," Cynthia said softly, clutching her cell phone in her hand. She shouldn't have come here. "I thought you said that he was awake and asking to speak with me. I thought it was about—"

Cynthia stopped talking, because she realized that it was no longer important.

"I wish you'd informed me of how critical the situation was." Cynthia was still staring at the closed elevator doors, various scenarios running through her mind as to how this could have gone differently had Jane Langston recognized her. "I wouldn't have agreed to—"

"Mr. Langston did wake up briefly, but it wasn't long after that he passed away. Why do you think it is he asked to speak with you?" Detective Nielsen gestured that they should take this to one of the alcoves that was set up for privacy. She gladly walked over to one of the blue leather seats that hadn't been designed for comfort. "Were the two of you still involved?"

Cynthia's first reaction was disgust, and she stared up at Detective Nielsen with shock. Did he think so little of her that he would assume she'd continue to have sex with a married man? Nausea had almost become a permanent fixture, so she didn't even bother to release the grip on her phone to rest a hand over her stomach.

"No, not at all," Cynthia answered bluntly, completely done with this discussion. She locked her knees together, fulling intending to stand and walk out of this hospital with her head held high. "Look, Detective, there's nothing more that I..."

Cynthia allowed her voice to trail off when Detective Nielsen knelt in front of her, blocking her from leaving her chair. His closeness was unexpected, and she drew back immediately.

What was happening?

Why was he...

Cynthia could only stare in horror as her mind registered the fact that he'd drawn his firearm from its holster and rested the cold metal against her knee. She sat motionless, as if she was frozen. The man before her no longer resembled the attentive police officer who was investigating a murder. He was trapping her in the seat and not letting her leave.

He was the killer.

Everything fell into place as Cynthia connected the facts.

The detective had access to the security cameras, he was privy to everything and anything related to Brad's murder in regard to alibis and opportunities given to friends and family, and he'd been able to manipulate the investigation with the simplest of fabrications.

"He had to go and fuck you, didn't he? Langston never could keep his dick in his pants." Detective Nielsen leaned forward so that their outward appearance was one of commiseration. The coldness in his dark eyes told her that he was most likely incapable of sympathy. "I'm going to need you to do exactly what I say without any trouble, Ms. Ellsworth."

Cynthia was still grappling with the fact that the man before her wasn't the detective she'd come to know over the past month. Honestly, a deep-seated fear had settled over her the instant he'd reached for his weapon.

The overwhelming need to escape had muddled her thoughts, but only temporarily until her anger surged forth and she wanted nothing more than to claw his eyes out for all that he'd put them through in his need for…

"Why?" Cynthia wasn't just stalling for time. She truly wanted to understand why Detective Nielsen would have killed Brad and tried to sabotage those who were closest to her. "Why would you do this?"

"As I said, we're going to stand up slowly before walking toward the stairwell."

The stairwell.

Did the stairs have security cameras?

Cynthia forced herself to take a deep breath, trying to focus on only one thing at a time—surviving being first on the list. She still had her cell phone in her hand, but he was watching her too closely for her to try and dial out.

The hospital had video surveillance everywhere, especially in the elevators, so there was no way in hell he would get away with abducting her here in the hospital and taking her somewhere else to kill. She'd been recorded upon her arrival, and there was no doubt a camera was pointed their way right this moment, which was the reason he'd kept his firearm next to her body.

A part of her understood that he could easily get rid of that evidence, as he'd done so before. She couldn't bring herself to accept that, though.

All she had to do was yell and struggle against his position and hopefully have her reaction recorded. Someone would see her dilemma, right? She didn't want to die, but she sure as hell wouldn't go down without leaving the evidence as to who was the guilty party.

"You need to remember something, Ms. Ellsworth. I have nothing to lose at this point. I'll shoot you right here if I have to." Nielsen leaned in a bit more, causing her to bend back slightly. She would never again think of him as someone with authority. "If you so much as act like something is wrong, I will make sure that you're not the only one I take out before I leave here."

Cynthia had no doubt he was telling her the truth. He was no longer the composed man who had taken lead in an investigation.

Nielsen had fooled them all.

"You could have gotten away with all of this had you not shown your hand here," Cynthia pointed out, trying to steady her voice. She failed. "No one knows anything yet. You and I can come to an agree—"

"It's too late for that, and you damn well know it." The ding of the elevator caused Cynthia's heart to race at the potential help that could save her, but she instantly changed her mind when he firmly pressed the barrel against her knee. "I will not hesitate to kill whoever comes out of that elevator if you make me."

Cynthia had a choice to make, but she wasn't willing to have someone else die because she panicked.

"You didn't have to tip your hand with me. I didn't know anything," Cynthia revealed a bit desperately, catching sight of a couple stepping off the elevator. She couldn't take the chance of them getting hurt. That didn't mean she couldn't cut some type of deal. "I still don't know anything. You let me go, and I'll pretend this never happened."

Nielsen lifted one side of his mouth up in mockery before shaking his head at her foolish attempt to escape this hospital unscathed.

"You don't expect me to believe that Langston asked for you the second he opened his eyes all because he wanted to apologize for lying to you?" Nielsen stood over her, holding his firearm alongside his pants so that it couldn't be seen from the foyer. "He came clean with you, didn't he? He told you the truth. He admitted to what Manon and Colbert did three years ago, and he confessed to what we were doing now."

"I still don't understand how you could be involved in this."

Nielsen didn't speak for what felt like an eternity, but Cynthia knew better. He was finally recognizing that she truly hadn't known what was going on until just now. Only it was too late, because he'd already tipped his hand by threatening her with his firearm.

"Detective, we can both walk away from this." Cynthia figured bargaining was her best chance to get out of this alive. She still wasn't one hundred percent positive that he was the one who had killed Brad. "It's clear that you've done something wrong, but I have no clue as to what that may be. So, we can—"

"Just stop it," Nielsen directed, rubbing his forehead as if he, too, was trying to come up with a solution. "I didn't want it to come to this. I truly didn't, but there isn't any way to go back. This was my mistake. I have no choice but to clean this mess up and move on."

"Then tell me why you did it," Cynthia asked quickly, hoping to buy some more time so she could figure out how she could get away without anyone else getting hurt. She gave a quick glance toward the elevator, noticing that the number above signified it had gone back down to the lobby. "I deserve to know, Detective."

"You make it sound like I wanted this to happen." Nielsen rested a hand on the arm of the chair, leaning in close. She didn't pull away this time, not willing to give him the satisfaction of seeing her physical fear. "You've got to understand. Manon, Colbert, and Langston basically promised me a fortune by investing in Langston's tech company. I was in over my head, caring for my mother and taking care of my entire family. Do you know how hard that is to do on a detective's salary? I pulled everything out of my retirement fund. I gambled it all on this one thing. It was supposed to be a sure thing. We were going to manipulate the stock price into going higher, and then Langston was going to present at some conference to give the illusion that something big was coming. The stock would have jumped, we would have sold our shares for a huge profit, and we'd have been set for life."

"What went wrong?" Cynthia barely got the words out, because it was clear she was running out of time. "Why kill Brad?"

"He needed to pull his money out early. The amount he'd invested...well, selling that amount of shares before the announcement would have tanked the price. All of our efforts would have been for nothing. One thing led to another, and..."

Nielsen gripped her upper arm until she had no choice but to stand. There was no odor of alcohol or rancid sweat. He was completely in control, and he had every intention of killing her and dumping her body like trash. "I'm done talking. I did what I had to do, and I plan on cleaning up the mess that was left behind."

They'd made all of this too easy for the detective. Marilyn, the other employees, and even Cynthia had kept Nielsen up-to-date practically twenty-four-seven with bits of information so that he'd always be one step ahead of all of them. It didn't help that Phil had been in the trenches, picking up crumbs of intel to pass on to the mastermind behind it all.

Before Nielsen could guide her toward the stairwell, his words resounded in her head.

"Clean up the mess?" Cynthia instinctively tried to pull away, but Nielsen tightened his grip. He'd even managed to pull her closer, but that didn't stop her from verbally asking him to confirm her suspicions. "You set up Grace to take the fall for Brad's murder. When that failed, you tried to set up her stepbrother because of their past. And you killed Kurt, because he was about to come clean about everything, wasn't he?"

"As I said, I'm done talking. And I'll give you a friendly reminder that I have nothing left to lose and everything to gain if this is handled right." Nielsen hid his firearm with the left side of his jacket, ensuring that she was also on his left side. One pull of the trigger and... "If you so much as give a sideways look to anyone in this hospital, there will be nothing stopping me from taking them out, too. What happens in the next few minutes rests on your shoulders. Are you willing to risk innocent lives of others just to save your own?"

CHAPTER EIGHTEEN

"MR. NICOLLET, I'M going to have to ask you to stay right where you are," Detective Mancini stated for the second time in the past thirty seconds. Gareth didn't give a shit what the man was demanding, because there was no way in hell he was remaining in the lobby of the hospital when Cynthia's life was in danger. "This is an ongoing investigation, and we don't want to tip our hand and endanger anyone unnecessarily."

"You and I both know that Cynthia is right outside of the ICU with Nielsen. You might be willing to leverage her life to get a conviction on a dirty cop, but I sure as hell am not." Gareth had never experienced such desperation as he did now, knowing full well that all access points to the ICU were currently blocked by police officers working with Internal Affairs. "Let me—"

"Look," Detective Mancini finally said with a bit of under-standing. Unfortunately, he hadn't changed his mind in regard to how he was going to play out the current situation. "I know how frustrating this is, but you need to let us do our jobs. You're more than likely to get Cynthia killed than you are to save her."

"Mancini, the elevators are clear."

The detective lifted a hand of acknowledgement to the on-scene Tactical Response Commander, keeping his focus on Gareth. Everything had spiraled out of control when he'd received a call on the way to the hospital from Smith, confirming that there was something going down with Cynthia in the mix. He'd gotten word from his father, but that was good enough for Gareth to corroborate his suspicions—Cynthia's life was in danger due to walking right into the middle of this mess.

Smith had the five-minute drive to explain that Mancini had been brought in from the State Police Special Investigation Division to assist with a review of one Fred Nielsen months ago. How all that came about, Gareth didn't understand and honestly didn't care. It became increasingly obvious with every passing minute that Mancini wanted to bring Nielsen in alive—as was his duty.

Gareth had already heard part of the plan when he'd made it through the hospital doors, right before another officer in tactical gear had blocked his access to the elevators. Law enforcement clearly expected Nielsen to take Cynthia to the roof of the building, possibly throwing her off the ledge, and making it seem as if she were too distraught to live after the death of her ex-lover.

At this point, Gareth didn't give a shit if the man lived or died. Let a sniper put one in the man's ear and be done with it.

"Detective Mancini, they're on the move," an officer said, gesturing for the police presence to vacate the immediate area. "Nielsen is bringing her down in the elevator now."

It was evident that Mancini hadn't believed Nielsen would parade Cynthia through the lobby, so something must have changed his mind—or someone.

"Detective, you realize the moment he sees you or the other officers that he'll take Cynthia as a hostage." Gareth was doing his best not to lose his shit, but he'd never quite been placed in this type of situation. The small box that held Cynthia's engagement ring practically burned a hole through his jacket. "Let me come between them and delay them from leaving the hospital."

"Three more floors, sir."

Mancini had to make a quick decision, and he finally opted for the only one available that didn't have Cynthia leaving the safety net that currently surrounded the building.

"You and I both know that she's dead if Nielsen gets her through those doors."

"And you're liable to join her six feet under if you blow this, hero."

Mancini quickly gave the hand gesture for those officers in view to take cover and blend into the background. He wasn't an ordinary detective with limited experience in field situations. From their earlier conversation, the man had been SID for fifteen years. His assignment to the local PD with Internal Affairs hadn't been his first, and his unit was known to do what was necessary to weed out the corruption within the ranks. Bottom line was that they closed cases.

Gareth had expected Mancini to drop back, but he remained steadfast as they both continued to walk toward the elevator bank.

"Follow my lead," Mancini directed under his breath, finally delivering on the promise that he was a man who knew what the hell he was doing. He had to be one hell of an actor, though. He could have easily made it in Hollywood. "And don't do anything stupid that could cost us our lives."

Gareth honestly didn't care about anything other than getting Cynthia away from Nielsen. How could a man throw away his integrity for money? Not only had he thrown away his honor, but he'd killed a man in cold blood for greed. Had he been so desperate that he didn't care about taking another man's life?

Nielsen's level of desperation was the motivating reason that Gareth needed to get Cynthia to safety before the man cracked.

"...so he confessed five minutes ago," Detective Mancini said as the doors slowly slid open to reveal a somewhat confident Nielsen holding Cynthia a little too close for comfort. "Can you imagine that? The guilt must have—"

Mancini broke off as he feigned surprise at finding Nielsen and Cynthia in the elevator. It took every ounce of mental fortitude for Gareth not to reach out and tear her away from Nielsen's side.

"Nielsen, perfect timing." Mancini held up his hands with what appeared to be a genuine smile of satisfaction. "Phil Colbert walked into the station ten minutes ago with his lawyer in tow. He actually said that he would confess to the murder of Brad Manon if the prosecutor would give him a plea. Can you believe that shit? I got your message that Langston was awake, so we'll need to talk with him about his involvement in this whole stock manipulation thing. I'll admit, I don't know shit about investments."

"K-Kurt's dead," Cynthia managed to say, clutching her phone and her purse against her stomach. Her gaze swung between Gareth and Detective Mancini, obviously believing they had no idea that Nielsen was holding her at gunpoint. Her palpable overwhelming terror had his heart pumping to the point of chest pain. "He didn't make it."

"I'm sorry to hear that." Mancini shook his head as if he were commiserating with her. "I doubt Langston's death will affect the outcome on this case, considering Colbert is willing to confess to everything. What a shame, though. I'm sure we'll contact you for a statement at some point, as well as everyone at Manon Investments. Detective Nielsen and I will be heading back to the station, but you—"

"Fuck!" Nielsen pulled up his firearm so fast that Cynthia didn't have time to react. Neither did Mancini. "Fuck! This wasn't supposed to go down like this, Rich. How the fuck did you know?"

Gareth had been fighting his own instincts this entire time not to do something foolish that could get Cynthia killed, but the situation had just escalated to light speed. Mancini had responded in kind, drawing his weapon and basically initiating a standoff.

There was only one problem.

The elevator doors were about to slide together, cutting off Gareth's ability to reach for Cynthia.

He couldn't allow that to happen.

How the hell had Nielsen been tipped off?

"Nobody move," Mancini instructed, though Gareth was pretty sure he was giving the directive to his subordinates. *Wait.* Someone had mentioned that the police were controlling the elevators. "Fred, it's over. You and I both know that I can't let you walk out of here with her. It's not going to happen."

Gareth had learned a lot in his years running the family's multiple foundations. One very valuable lesson was to allow the experts to do their job. He wasn't a doctor, so he didn't give anyone medical advice. He wasn't a lawyer, which meant he referred all legal matters to the professionals. A police officer? He sure as hell wasn't even remotely qualified—which meant he had no choice but to trust in Mancini.

Gareth caught Cynthia's gaze to somehow try and reassure her that everything was going to be fine. It was then that he realized how calm and composed Cynthia actually was in this scenario.

That scared the hell out of him more than any firearm.

She always did like to take matters into her hands and lead the bull, but this was different.

Her life was on the line.

His life.

She was his everything.

She wouldn't do something to—

Everything happened at once. Cynthia lifted her right leg and slammed the back of her high heel down onto Nielsen's shoe with all her might, while shifting to the side and bringing her elbow up at the same time to smash it into the underside of his nose. Nielsen might have been expecting Mancini or even Gareth himself to make a foolish move, but Cynthia had outsmarted all of them.

She rushed forward, straight into Gareth's waiting arms at the precise time a shot rang out. The explosive reverberation echoed in the sterile foyer of the hospital, though neither he nor Cynthia had seen who pulled the trigger on their weapon—he'd immediately shielded her from harm by engulfing her in his embrace while turning his body away so that his back was toward the standoff.

"Cuff him. Read him his rights, then get a damned doctor down here now!"

Gareth glanced over his shoulder to find Mancini holstering his weapon while two uniformed police officers were kneeling over Nielsen. He was holding his right shoulder with an expression of pain, but it was clear that he'd finally given up.

"Ms. Ellsworth, are you alright?" Mancini had come up to the two of them as if this was just another day at the office. That was doubtful, considering the fact that Gareth had read the statistics regarding the low percentage an officer actually drew his firearm during his career. Again, the collective display of composure was outstanding. "Did he hurt you?"

"No," Cynthia replied after clearing her throat a couple of times. Her blue eyes were dark from the adrenaline rushing through her veins. The way she was clutching his arm told him that she was still in fight mode. "I'm fine. But Nielsen admitted to killing Brad Manon and Kurt Langston. He—"

"Good. We have all the evidence we need to put Nielsen away for a very long time, but your statement will solidify the case. That was nice work, Ms. Ellsworth. This could have ended a lot differently had you not acted with those outstanding self-defense moves." Mancini nodded toward another man, though it wasn't a uniformed officer. "You got this? I'm going to take Ms. Ellsworth's statement. You can…"

Gareth took this opportunity to gently take Cynthia's beautiful face into the palms of his hands. He was shaking from all the adrenaline, but he didn't give two shits about who saw his reaction. He'd come too close to losing her to care what anyone else thought of him.

"Don't you ever do that again," Gareth whispered desperately, searching her gaze for confirmation that she was okay. She'd been held at gunpoint. One mistake could have killed her. "I mean it, Cyn. You are everything I need in this world."

"Is that why there's a ring box in your jacket?" Cynthia was smiling brightly, telling him that her adrenaline was still pumping at a high level. She would come down eventually, and he would be there for her. If this lightheartedness was to keep herself together, then he'd follow suit. He'd do anything for her. "Is that why we were having lunch at our favorite restaurant? I'm sorry I didn't make it. I got a little distracted with catching the killer and all."

Gareth couldn't help but laugh, though he sounded more like a lunatic than the man the hospital staff was hauling away on a gurney to the ER. A glint of light bounced off the metal handcuffs, telling a story all on its own.

"Ms. Ellsworth, this is where I need to reintroduce myself," Detective Mancini interrupted, either not knowing or caring that they were in the middle of a private conversation. He had a case to close, and Gareth was more than willing and happy to continue to divulge such intimate feelings later when he and Cynthia were alone. "I actually work for the State Police SID assigned to assist the local Internal Affairs department, and I have been investigating Fred Nielsen for quite some time."

"That's why you met with Smith in private the other day." Cynthia was connecting the dots that Gareth already had time to link together. He had released her from his grasp enough so that she could face the detective, though they both kept ahold of each other's hands. "You were hoping that he would have more information that could lead you to an arrest while Nielsen was busy elsewhere."

"Honestly, I was working every angle I could," Detective Mancini confessed with an unapologetic shrug. "Nielsen cashing out his retirement fund early to invest in a tech firm raised a lot of eyebrows early on. As we all know, that's not a crime in and of itself. With that said, a rookie overhead a phone conversation that I'm not at liberty to disclose. At least, not until this case goes to trial, but it got the ball rolling. I'm sure you get the rest."

"Were you brought in before Brad's death?" Cynthia asked, a slight tremor in her voice finally making itself known. Her adrenaline was finally starting to fade. Gareth wrapped his arm around her and held her close. "Or after?"

"Before, but you can understand how everything began to unravel from there. Why don't we find a seat, and you can start from the beginning?" Detective Mancini must have been able to secure a private room, because he began walking toward an officer who was standing in an open doorway that led to what appeared to be a small conference room. "Phil, could you grab some coffee for me and Mr. Nicollet and a water for Ms. Ellsworth?"

"Please, call me Cynthia. And thank you for remembering that I don't drink coffee."

The last thing Gareth needed was caffeine after all they'd gone through today, but he also wouldn't turn the stuff down. The next few hours were going to be a rather rough crash, especially given Cynthia's need to testify against Nielsen in the inevitable murder trial.

Mancini stepped to the side to allow Gareth and Cynthia to enter the room first.

"Did I mention how proud I am of you?" Gareth held out a chair for Cynthia, who was looking down at her high heels. The very shoe that might have saved her life. "A lot of people would have been frozen in fear. But not you, Cyn. You kept it together and saved everyone involved."

"Are you kidding?" Cynthia lifted one side of her red lips that hadn't faded in the least as she continued to amaze him on every level. "I saw the odd-shaped box in your jacket and realized what you had planned. I wasn't going to miss that for the world. Oh, and I expect a do-over. I want the whole nine yards."

"I love you."

What more could he say?

His life would never have a dull moment.

"I love you, too, Gareth Nicollet." Cynthia glanced down her legs once more in admiration. "And for the record, I love these heels."

CHAPTER NINETEEN

One month later…

"THIS ISN'T SO bad for hell," Grace said as she slowly spun in a circle, taking in the large trading room that would eventually become Gallo Capital Management. It was still bare bones, with nothing to see but the drywall and cement floor. The potential for their upcoming office space was beyond exciting. "I think I can stay awhile."

"We might have ended up here, but please don't jinx us," Laurel responded with a laugh, still carrying the bottle of red merlot she'd brought with her after Smith had given her the keys to show the office space to Cynthia and Grace. "I think we've had enough excitement this year. Wouldn't you two agree?"

Cynthia totally agreed, but she remained silent as she continued to walk through the empty office space. It was smaller than what Brad and Paul had rented for Manon Investments, but that choice had been made with a purpose. This more intimate setting made for a better working environment, especially after such distrust had been left behind with all the recriminations.

Laurel and Grace took a seat on a plank of wood left behind by some of the workers. They continued their conversation about the events of the past couple of months, giving Cynthia time to explore her new work environment at her leisure.

A fresh start was what everyone needed, and this space was

perfect.

Gareth was due back into town this evening, and they'd set aside the weekend to go house hunting. She didn't want to be too far from the city, so they'd narrowed their search down to a few surrounding neighborhoods. She'd even chosen around eight properties for them to comb through first.

But they would have to wait until tomorrow.

Tonight was all theirs.

"...trial date. The SEC is now involved, but Smith has given them everything they needed and more in relation to what happened." Laurel must have sensed that Cynthia had come back into the trading area, because she was holding up a plastic glass filled with wine. "Greed is a powerful motivator. We deal with it every day, but Fred Nielsen clearly let desperation take hold where common sense should have won out."

Cynthia gratefully took the wine, but she couldn't spend another minute of discussing Fred Nielsen or Phil Colbert. Brad had been no better, but again, no one deserved to die in such a fashion.

"Ladies, we have bright futures ahead of us," Cynthia reminded them as they both scooted over to give her room on the plank of wood. "Talk to me. What's been happening with the two of you lately?"

Their professional careers weren't the only thing that had changed recently. Grace had officially moved in with Rye, Laurel and Smith had set a wedding date in the summer, and Cynthia had gotten engaged to the man she wanted to spend her life with—a man typified by honor, compassion, and loyalty.

It so helped that he respected her love of high heels.

She glanced down, just now realizing that she was wearing the black high heels that always brought her luck. Technically, her burgundy heels had lived up to the challenge as well, but her current choice spoke volumes for the weekend ahead.

"My mom and Smith's mother have basically taken over the wedding plans, but I'm more than okay with that." Laurel sipped her wine and continued to talk about locations, the size of the guest list, and more importantly the color scheme. "It's taken up so much of our time, though, and I miss this. Us. I love our wine powwows."

"You just love the wine," Grace countered with a grin. "Be honest."

Laurel bumped shoulders with Grace in response before shooting a smile toward Cynthia.

"What about you? I'm surprised that your left bicep isn't larger than your right, considering the size of that engagement ring."

"I think she's just obsessed with his large—"

"Enough," Cynthia replied with a laugh, kicking off her high heels and settling in for the second bottle that Laurel thought she'd snuck into the new office space in that tote bag of hers. "I missed this, too."

They'd all been through a lot these past two months, both in their professional and personal lives. One thing had always held steady, though. And that deserved a toast.

Cynthia held up her wineglass, waiting for Grace and Laurel to follow suit. The plastic cups didn't clink the way their usual crystal glasses did in their salutes, but the fundamental meaning was still the same.

Their bond was unbreakable.

"To friendship."

~ THE END ~

Thank you so much for reading the Office Roulette trilogy! Did you know that the Keys to Love series is about to come to an end with the last two books releasing soon—Unlocking Shadows and Unlocking Darkness? This small town romantic suspense will keep you guessing, so click below to the series page and read all about it!

Keys to Love Series

www.kennedylayne.com/keys-to-love-series.html

Their homecoming wasn't so welcoming. Four brothers and one sister each gave twelve years of their lives to serve their country and fulfill their family's legacy of service. As each of them return to their home of record, they weren't prepared for what awaited them—an unforgivable sin that has been hidden for twelve long years. Secrets and lies are concealed in the dark shadows of the very town they were raised in, and the Kendall family will have no choice but to rely on one another to unravel the sinister evil that they all hold the keys to unlock.

Books by Kennedy Layne

Office Roulette Series
Means (Office Roulette, Book One)
Motive (Office Roulette, Book Two)
Opportunity (Office Roulette, Book Three)

Keys to Love Series
Unlocking Fear (Keys to Love, Book One)
Unlocking Secrets (Keys to Love, Book Two)
Unlocking Lies (Keys to Love, Book Three)
Unlocking Shadows (Keys to Love, Book Four)
Unlocking Darkness (Keys to Love, Book Five)

Surviving Ashes Series
Essential Beginnings (Surviving Ashes, Book One)
Hidden Ashes (Surviving Ashes, Book Two)
Buried Flames (Surviving Ashes, Book Three)
Endless Flames (Surviving Ashes, Book Four)
Rising Flames (Surviving Ashes, Book Five)

CSA Case Files Series
Captured Innocence (CSA Case Files 1)
Sinful Resurrection (CSA Case Files 2)
Renewed Faith (CSA Case Files 3)
Campaign of Desire (CSA Case Files 4)
Internal Temptation (CSA Case Files 5)
Radiant Surrender (CSA Case Files 6)
Redeem My Heart (CSA Case Files 7)

About the Author

First and foremost, I love life. I love that I'm a wife, mother, daughter, sister… and a writer.

I am one of the lucky women in this world who gets to do what makes them happy. As long as I have a cup of coffee (maybe two or three) and my laptop, the stories evolve themselves and I try to do them justice. I draw my inspiration from a retired Marine Master Sergeant that swept me off of my feet and has drawn me into a world that fulfills all of my deepest and darkest desires. Erotic romance, military men, intrigue, with a little bit of kinky chili pepper (his recipe), fill my head and there is nothing more satisfying than making the hero and heroine fulfill their destinies.

Thank you for having joined me on their journeys…

Email:

kennedylayneauthor@gmail.com

Facebook:

facebook.com/kennedy.layne.94

Twitter:

twitter.com/KennedyL_Author

Website:

www.kennedylayne.com

Newsletter:

www.kennedylayne.com/newslettertext.html